A DEATH AT EASTWICK

L. C. WARMAN

greenleaf &
plympton

Address:
Greenleaf & Plympton
P.O. Box 36621
18640 Mack Ave.
Grosse Pointe Farms, MI 48236-9998

Greenleaf & Plympton is a publisher of gothic books, both classic and modern. To see our full catalog, visit www.greenleafandplympton.com.

Cover art: Caroline Teagle Johnson

Proofreading: Alexandra Ott

Library of Congress Control Number: 2019944385

ISBN (e-book) 978-1-950103-14-0

ISBN (print) 978-1-950103-15-7

CHAPTER 1

*J*ohn Eastwick Sr. died before the scandal hit.

His son, John Eastwick Jr. first heard the news of his father's death on a Tuesday morning. He was sitting in the light-filled undergraduate library at Montvale, watching a group of bright-eyed tourists snapping photos of one of the prestigious college's ivy-strewn yards, when his mother called.

"You have to come home," were her first words.

His father, she explained, had died in his bathtub. An aneurysm, or heart attack, or something catastrophic and quick. By the time Mrs. Eastwick had checked on him, it was too late.

It was a few hours' plane ride from Montvale's east-coast, seaside campus to the wooded, lakeside town of St. Clair. John Jr. spent most of it in a stupor, holding his history course book in front of him with a green highlighter in one hand, high-lighting everything because his mind could focus on nothing. *Death*. It felt like a bad joke.

John spent the next week in a zombie-like trance, next to his weeping mother, sorting through condolence cards, calling back lawyers and business associates, and making what seemed like insane decisions about caskets and flowers and suits until his father had been buried in the family plot in the St. Clair cemetery, and the only remaining John Eastwick returned with his mother to their family estate.

The speed of it all had shocked John, who had never buried a close family member in his twenty-one years of life. His grandparents had passed away before he was born or when he was too young to remember, and the small size of the rest of his family meant that he had been one semester away from becoming a college graduate with no real experience of death or grief.

Indeed, John had had a blessed life before his father's sudden death: he was, beyond all measure, rich, and besides that good-looking, athletic enough to play two varsity sports in high school (one of them well), and above six feet. He had taken prestigious internship after prestigious internship at various financial firms during the summers in between college, and had spent his winters with his family skiing in the Swiss Alps or, when his mother wanted something "easier and less of a fuss," in Aspen.

Perhaps due to the influence of his parents, who stressed hard work, honesty, and integrity, John did not grow up into the monster one might expect with so many advantages. He was made to feel keenly how lucky he was and to work to deserve (impossible as it was) such an unequal portion in life. He was, naturally, a little spoiled, but he was unfailingly polite, acceptably modest, and rigidly scrupulous.

But tragedy rarely strikes in isolation. And two days before John's uncle, aunt, and cousin arrived for the reading of his father's will, the scandal broke.

And John Eastwick Sr. was plastered across every newspaper and social media feed in the nation.

CHAPTER 2

"It's a mistake, of course," John said to his mother.

They were seated at the table in his parents' master bedroom, inside a little breakfast nook that gathered streaming sunshine from the east-facing windows. His mother was dressed in her morning robe, her face scrubbed clean and her hair tied back, looking youthful and small and slim as her hands fluttered over the paper.

"Mom?" John said, when Mrs. Eastwick did not respond.

She looked up at him. Mrs. Eastwick was fifty-four, a good five years younger than her recently passed husband. She was normally cheerful, scatterbrained, and sometimes frivolous, though she could occasionally draw her attention to some important task and apply herself with admirable dedication. For instance, the raising of her son: Mrs. Eastwick was a most attentive mother, the kind who made spreadsheets of her son's activities and read parenting books in her spare time—of which she had much, given that her husband's income had enabled the Eastwicks to maintain a robust household staff. Her son was her greatest pride, and her biggest accomplishment had been to let him go: to not be the kind of mother who fretted and fussed and called him every day, whining for him to return home or begging him to join some family business so she could keep a closer watch on him. Mrs. Eastwick had been proud of herself for that. Now, she felt ill.

"It must be a mistake," Mrs. Eastwick repeated faintly.

"Dad would never do something like that," John said. But he was watching his mother's expression closely. "Neither of you would."

Mrs. Eastwick swallowed and looked down at the papers. *College Bribery Scandal.* Now, that just sounded so very crude. Of course Mr. Eastwick would never *bribe* anyone. He was the most honest man who had ever lived. He had run a very powerful business for thirty years, and men like that lived lives that were open to great scrutiny—and Mr. Eastwick had passed all of it. Never once had an employee, a business associate, a former colleague said a bad word about him.

"A mistake," Mrs. Eastwick repeated. "He made a donation. But not a *bribe.*"

Yes, she remembered how he had brought it up to her a few years ago. It hadn't raised any red flags, though of course it must have been unusual if she still remembered it. A donation—a donation to Montvale, Mr. Eastwick's alma mater, specifically to a coach on the crew team.

"The crew team?" Mrs. Eastwick had asked. (She must have asked! Of course she would have asked.)

"Well," Mr. Eastwick would have said—for Mrs. Eastwick couldn't remember, though she could picture him pinching one corner of his mustache in the way that he always did, a twinkle in his eye—"Well, yes. Why not? They could use it."

Why not indeed? And their son was applying to school soon—surely a donation like that couldn't hurt his chances. John had good grades, but so did every high school student these days. Surely if Montvale could see that John's father was a very *engaged* alum, well, they might think twice before chucking his application into the reject pile. Besides, that was nothing unusual, wasn't it? Surely the rich had certain backdoors like this, and always had. Mrs. Eastwick hadn't grown up rich, so who was she to understand the unfathomable, the myriad ways in which privilege plucked and slithered and winked its way through life?

"What donation?" John said, coloring. "You mean the ones he made every year?"

"It was for the crew team."

"But did he make it out to Montvale? Or to"—and here John referenced the paper—"the Blunderbloot Association?"

"What's the Blunderbloot Association?"

"The charity. The fake one, that was bribing college officials in return for their help admitting students."

Mrs. Eastwick ran a hand over her face. She was very tired, and it seemed awfully rude of the paper to publish something like this, make her deal with something like this, so soon after her husband's death. There were forty-nine other names on the list—couldn't they have left off Mr. Eastwick's?

"I'm confused," Mrs. Eastwick said.

John, with much too much patience, slid the article over to her. "Parents gave money to this charity. The charity bribed school officials—coaches, admissions counselors, professors— to get the kids in. But Dad never donated to the charity, right? He donated to the school, every year. So why would he even need to do something like that?" John gave a short, nervous laugh.

"We donated to a lot of charities, darling. I can't be sure—"

"It's important, Mom. Can you look it up? Maybe we can call the journalist right away—our lawyer, too. Correct this as soon as possible." Luckily, a few actresses from old sitcoms and a pop singer from a boy band with hits from the 80s were also in the group of fifty names, and thus far they, as the most recognizable faces, had received the majority of the press coverage. But that wouldn't last forever, and besides, even now John's father's name was being maligned across the nation. All of his former associates, all of his friends, all of their family, would see it and assume that John Eastwick Sr. was guilty.

Mrs. Eastwick sighed and rose. She went to the family laptop, kept in the kitchen nook, which was always the one used most often, even though both husband and wife kept giant offices in the west wing of the house. She bit her lip and clicked away on the keyboard. "Tax returns, tax returns," she murmured.

"Command 'F' to search," John said, walking over to peer over her shoulder. Mrs. Eastwick did not like that. She felt a pit in her stomach, though of course her husband couldn't have been caught up in some silly plot such as this. Of course he wouldn't...not *John*...

"B-l-u-n-d," John spelled.

Mrs. Eastwick typed. Then paused. Both mother and son leaned closer to the screen.

The donation was for $100,000. It was in the tax return from three years before, when John had been applying to colleges.

CHAPTER 3

On the other side of St. Clair, in a trendy modern ranch home located within walking distance to one of St. Clair's lakeside parks, the other Eastwick family sat down to a gleeful and excited breakfast.

"Didn't know he had it in him!" Edward Eastwick, younger brother of the late John Eastwick Sr. said maliciously, straightening out the newspaper with a *crack*. "Well, what do you know! Good old goodie two shoes, breaking the law. Bribing! It's bribery, Vanessa."

Vanessa Eastwick's lips curled, highlighting the fine wrinkles around her plum lipstick. She reached for the cream and poured some into her coffee without giving her husband a response. Vanessa was the exact opposite of Edward in a number of ways: she was thin where he was fat, flaxen- and fair-haired where he was dark-haired and hairy, endowed with a supreme overabundance of chin and nose where he was lacking the former and had not much of the latter—just a round bulb squashed flatly to his face. Growing up, Edward Eastwick had always been the "less than" of the two Eastwick brothers, for of course everyone had to compare them: Edward was less handsome, less agreeable, less athletic, and

7

less intelligent. But such unpleasant circumstances had not created a humble man prepared for the cruelties of the world: instead, they had fashioned a man quick to take offense, primed to discover a slight, and ready to consider each and every new acquaintance as a potential enemy.

Their son, Michael, drew out his own copy of the paper, which he had walked down to the nearest café to procure. Michael was nearer his mother in looks and personality—that is, better at moving in polite society and slower to lose his temper. "Could it be wrong?" Michael said. "Uncle John did donate a lot to Montvale."

"Guess he didn't think that was enough," Edward Eastwick said, tugging at the loose skin of his jowls. His eyes were twinkling. "I never donated a penny to get you in anywhere, Michael my boy! All your own merit."

"I'm sure if we were rich enough, you would have," Michael said dryly, flipping the newspaper. Michael had graduated from a small fine arts college out east, and was on his fifth year working as a film and movie critic—or so said his business card, as he technically still lived with his parents, and wrote freelance articles on the side.

"How embarrassed Elizabeth must be," Vanessa Eastwick said. She watched her husband as he perused the paper, taking another sip of her coffee. Reading gave her headaches, but gossiping had great salutary effects.

"Quite! Embarrassed as can be!' Edward exclaimed.

"Should I give her a call? Comfort her?"

"Perhaps. Ask how she's taking it. And John Jr., too! Remember how he gloated to us when he got in?"

"Well, they certainly made a point to call us immediately," Vanessa said, sniffing. She and Elizabeth had gone to school together, had been, in fact, great friends once upon a time. It was Vanessa who started dating Edward Eastwick first, and through Vanessa that Elizabeth met and married John Eastwick Sr. At the time it had seemed so fortuitous—two best friends marrying two brothers, to unite them in friendship and family forever. The subsequent years had taught Vanessa how naïve such a belief was.

"We'll see them in two days anyway," Michael said, straightening. "We don't have to call them now."

"It would be rude to bring it up in front of other company," Vanessa said, and so reasoning, dialed. Her face fell a few seconds later, and she placed the phone back on the table, deflating.

"No answer?" Edward said. "Call again, my dear! Perhaps she didn't hear it."

"She'll call me back," Vanessa said, sniffing. She took the paper from Edward and leaned back, making a show of becoming quite interested in the contents. "I'm not desperate to talk to her."

"Hmph!" said Edward. He made eye contact with Michael and winked. "Well, might be a little more interesting to see your cousin now, eh? I wonder if he'll go back to that fancy school."

"Probably not," Michael said, and if he ever came even marginally close to pitying John Eastwick, it was then.

CHAPTER 4

Two days passed in various states of disquiet, unease, and dread by the widow and surviving son of John Eastwick Sr. The pair had plenty to worry about in terms of memorial service preparations, and more than enough to talk about to steer their conversations away from the college incident, as John Jr. had come to think of it.

In fact, he felt fairly certain that he and his mother would just never talk of it again. This both relieved and annoyed him —at times he wanted to grab her by the shoulders and demand that she answer him, explain how his father (his father! his kind, wonderful, inexpressibly perfect father!) had gotten wrapped up in something like this. Other times he wanted to erase the whole memory from his head altogether, wanted to let himself believe that something was afoul. Indeed, there were times in those days when he convinced himself that sinister business *was* afoot. His father had enemies, and it was possible that someone, for some reason, would have delighted in framing him.

The day of the funeral had been terrible, cold and windswept. A long church service was followed by a freezing burial, followed again by an uncomfortable wake. The funeral had been torture for John: he had teared up half a dozen times, had stammered his way through an emotional speech, and had held his mother while she sobbed into his shoulder through the better part of his father being lowered into the earth. It was like an awful movie, gray-toned and depressing, that he could not escape from.

The wake, undoubtedly, was the worst of all. The thin shell of protection that had existed around John and his mother during the funeral seemed to lift at the wake; everyone seemed to want to step forward and pull them close for a hug, or press their hands and tell them just how devastatingly sorry they were about everything. John had to keep it together as people cried to him about how much they would miss his father, or worse, as they shook his hand jovially and said something glib about his father looking down on him and smiling.

But that had all been *before*, when John still had not known about the college incident. Now, facing a memorial service with that in the back of his mind, knowing that everyone he met would have seen the headlines—it was absolute torture. He begged his mother to cancel it, but she was, for once, absolutely firm. "We're not going to hide," she said. "Besides, people want to pay their respects."

And so John found himself standing in the house that evening, doing his best to smile at every newcomer, to nod and thank them for their well wishes, to reassure them that everything would be alright (that was the one thing he had not expected—how much he had to reassure everyone else that all would be okay).

"How are you holding up?" a woman said, squeezing John's elbow. He tensed until he turned and saw who it was, and then smiled wearily.

"Ms. Jenkins," he said. "How are you?"

"You're well old enough to call me Annette," she said, smiling back. His father's lawyer wore a slim-fitting, elegant dress with black-and-white stripes, and her hair was coiled back in a tight bun. She couldn't have been past forty, with liquid brown eyes, ebony skin, and long, elegant features, from her thin hands to her high neck.

"Let's say we get a drink?" Annette suggested. John was more than happy to comply, and they skirted around the edge of the room, maneuvering deftly through people who called John's name or tried to open yet another mournful conversation with him.

"This is torture," John said as they entered his kitchen. His mother had thought a memorial service at the house would be the easiest and best way to do it, and John had agreed at the time—though now he realized that by doing so, he could never escape these people, not until they decided to leave.

"It will be over soon. Luke, could we have two old-fashioneds? Extra cherries in mine, please."

The chef, a tall and broad-shouldered man of thirty-eight or thirty-nine, did not answer her, nor did he look up. But he moved quickly to comply.

Annette and John exchanged niceties: they had both been very well, thank you, and their respective families were (other than the obvious) as well as could be. John felt a flash of heat whenever he spoke of college and bristled for the question, but Annette asked him only about his mother and the reading of the will, to take place at eight p.m. Annette herself was as enigmatic as always: she had come on a junior associate fifteen years ago, apprenticing herself to John Eastwick Sr.'s previous lawyer, and had quickly won the affection and loyalty of John's father. She spoke little of her family or outside life: sometimes John thought this was because she was intensely private, and other times John wondered if this was because there was nothing to speak of, and if Annette had devoted herself so whole-heartedly to her career that she had nothing left to give.

Luke returned with the old-fashioneds, mumbling his condolences to John as he slid them over the white-granite countertop. Luke had been with them almost as long as

Annette; he was as large as a mountain and as silent as one, too. He was stiff and formal with outsiders and was only really at ease with John's mother Elizabeth, given they had spent the most time together in menu planning, shopping, and the like. Now he ran one hand nervously over his blond-red hair, pulled back into a low ponytail, and glanced over at Annette, who raised her glass to him in a silent cheers.

"Thanks," Annette said, setting the drink on the counter. She seemed distracted for a moment, eyes on Luke, and did not take a sip. "You've always made a mean drink."

Luke first looked surprised, then bewildered, then blushed crimson and turned.

Annette led them back into the mansion's ballroom, with an apologetic glance at John. "The sooner you finish your appearances, the sooner it will all be over," she said. "Have you spoken to your aunt and uncle? And cousin Mike, was it?"

"We've said hello."

"That's nice," Annette said. Her eyes scanned the room, locking on the trio after just a few seconds' search. "They look just as miserable as you to be here."

Indeed, Uncle Edward, Aunt Vanessa, and his cousin Michael looked like a small army that had closed ranks, sour faces turned towards one another, shoulders spinning to rebuff anyone who tried to break in. Just now it looked as though Tatiana, John Eastwick Sr.'s secretary, was making her attempt. She was a tall, statuesque woman of thirty, pale and striking, her arms covered in gold bracelets and her ice-blonde hair fastened smartly into the French braid that John had always seen her wearing. He felt a pang of sympathy for her as she colored at the slight, and turned away. Tatiana had always been kind to him, in all her seven years of service. Soon enough she turned away and floated into the kitchen, cheeks red, perhaps for a drink or to regroup.

"She's coming to the reading of the will, you know," Annette said.

"Tatiana is?"

"Yes, and Luke. I just read the newest version today. Your father was generous to all of his employees, but a few more than others."

He could feel Annette searching his face and blushed. He had had enough of a shock over the last few days about what his father had done: he didn't need to add any conjectures or rumors to his headspace. "Great," John said curtly. "I'm sure she was a great secretary to him."

Annette took the hint. She talked of other things—of old colleagues, of St. Clair gossip, of real estate prices. John listened as best he could, murmuring assent in some places, giving a well-timed "Mmmm" in others. All the while, though, his eyes kept sliding back to his uncle. He couldn't be imagining it: every so often, he would catch the older man's eye, and John could have sworn he saw pure malice in it.

CHAPTER 5

*A*nnette strode back into the kitchen fifteen minutes later. Luke floated nearer, pretending to wipe down one of the countertops.

"How goes the catering?" Annette said, glancing at the line of discarded cheese and appetizer plates that were lined up next to the industrial-sized sink in the Eastwick's second kitchen.

"Well enough," Luke said stiffly. "The samosas were popular. How's the event?"

Annette sighed and slid into one of the barstools at the counter. Luke stood in front of her, scrubbing at a nonexistent spot just inches from where her arms were draped. Annette wanted very much to rest her forehead on her hands and just sleep, just get the next few days over with. Losing Mr. Eastwick at such a time—it was enough to make her knees buckle. And there was so much that she had been planning, so much that sat so precariously now…

"Are you sure I should come to the reading?" Luke asked, lowering his voice. "It isn't…it isn't a little suspicious?"

"Why should it be suspicious?" Annette asked sharply, and Luke winced, stepping back. He was too sensitive sometimes, she thought, a bitter edge slicing through her. She knew she was being unfair, but then, why shouldn't she be? "You're in the will—substantially. You should be there."

Luke looked uncomfortable. "But why would he single us out? And Tatiana? Surely there were others that—"

"He singled us out because we did a great job for him. For his family. Don't be paranoid."

"You, maybe. You worked with him so often. And Tatiana, Tatiana must have been with him all the time. But me…"

"You've been with the family for years."

"So have many others."

Annette suppressed the urge to roll her eyes. "What are you worried about, Luke?"

"Never mind."

"No, go on. Seriously, what is it?"

Luke hesitated. "I just…if he knew that…I wouldn't want him to be so generous if he realized that I—"

"You are being absolutely *ridiculous*," Annette said, checking over her shoulder. She took a deep breath. This was always a problem for her. She got angry, she said things she didn't mean, she scoffed when people tried to tell her things she felt were absolutely ridiculous. She had told herself that this time it would be different, that this time—for good reason —she would control her temper. "Luke. Seriously. Don't worry about it. Of all the things wrong with it, well, that's the least of my worries right now."

The door to the kitchen burst open. Tatiana strode in, face blotchy with red and white patches, hands shaking slightly by her sides. She stopped short seeing Luke and Annette, her eyes narrowing slightly as she folded her arms and leaned up against the far wall. "Am I interrupting?" she said.

"Not at all," Annette replied lightly, as Luke moved— much too quickly, Annette thought—to another part of the kitchen, making a show of putting away the dishes. "How's everything going?"

"I'm sick of this place," Tatiana spat. Annette braced; she had rarely seen Mr. Eastwick's capable, hard-working secretary so flustered. "I want to get out of here."

"You're coming to the reading, though?"

"Obviously."

Annette nodded. Something about the secretary felt electric, almost dangerous. Tatiana seemed to feel her gaze and scowled.

"Please," Tatiana said. "Go back to your conversation. Don't let me interrupt."

Luke dropped a dish that went clattering into the sink, the crash echoing across the kitchen.

Tatiana smirked. "Good luck with it," Tatiana said to Annette, her eyes flashing. "Whatever it is, I hope it's been worth it. Because it won't work out." The final words were almost a challenge, and then Tatiana pushed herself off of the wall and left the room.

Annette's heart stuttered a step. *She knows*, the lawyer thought, her hand fluttering to her throat. *She knows*.

CHAPTER 6

*E*lizabeth Eastwick tired as the night passed on. By the end of it, she could barely summon a pale smile for the guests that pressed her hands and assured her that "John was such a good man" and that "at least he's not suffering now."

"Oh, I hope not!" Elizabeth would say, and the guests would give her a funny look and struggle to come up with another platitude.

This death business, Elizabeth decided, was entirely unwholesome. How cruel that people had to deal with it! She, like her son, had not experienced much of it—her parents had passed on when she was in her early thirties, one after the other, and of course at the time it had felt like the end of the world. But they had been ill, too; there had been warnings; she had had time to nurse them, to cry at the doctors' offices, to say goodbye. This kind of death, so sudden and unexpected, was like having the carpet ripped out from under her, like reaching the top of the stairs only to tumble head over heels back down. She didn't like it; she didn't like it at all.

"Ready?" John said, joining her. Elizabeth jumped. How like his father her son looked in this light! If his hair was a

21

little grayer, his figure a little looser, perhaps.... Ah. Ghosts and shadows, Elizabeth thought, and gave her son a smile that seemed to puzzle him.

"Where are we going?" Elizabeth asked, taking her son's arm. The guests were almost out now; the final ones remaining seemed to be taking the hint, grabbing the last few shrimp off of the platter and downing their drinks on their way out. *Goodbye, vultures!* Elizabeth wanted to shout, waving one hand. *Toodle-oo!* The thought of it almost made her giggle.

"We're going to the reading," John said gently. "Remember? You wanted it tonight?"

"Ah. I suppose I did, hmm?"

"It won't take long."

Dear, lovely John. She really didn't deserve him, she knew that. She wasn't the kind of mother who should have ended up with such an upstanding, smart, kind, dutiful son as John. She was the kind of mother who forgot to pack a morning snack for her son, who wasn't able to help him with his math homework past fourth grade (more out of fear than lack of knowledge), who second-guessed herself at every turn, from what vitamins her dear boy should be taking to whether it really was wise for him to go to that summer class in Spain. She had been forgetful, doubting, baffled most of the time— and still he had turned out radiantly. John Sr. was to thank for that, though her husband had vehemently disagreed with her whenever she had said it. *It's all you,* John Sr. would say, taking Elizabeth's hands in his. And the thing was, each time he said it, she believed him!

They entered the library. It had always been an almost holy place for Elizabeth, one she did not dare enter too often. It was where John Sr. had spent a good deal of his time, choosing the stately room with its floor-to-ceiling bookshelves over his light and airy office in the front with the windows that gave a view of the front grounds. Her eyes passed over the green and gold volumes, the human-sized globe set atop the wooden platform at the far end, next to a sliding ladder and a wooden bench with a set of apothecary glasses atop them (once, John Sr. had filled them all with candy in a fit of whimsy, which had lasted until John Jr. toppled the largest over, and ended up in a pile of glass and toffees). She saw Tatiana sitting at the bench, a glass of red wine in one hand, her bright eyes unfocused. When she caught Elizabeth looking at her, she straightened and scowled, lifting her head high. Elizabeth turned away, letting her son direct her to a high-backed chair adjacent to the couch he nestled into. Annette was already seated opposite, in another chair, the will in an envelope on her lap.

It did not take the others long to filter in. The lights in the library were orange and dim; Annette rose twice to try to brighten them, to no effect. The result was that the shadows in the room multiplied and twisted, so that by the time Edward, Vanessa, Michael, and Luke had seated themselves, over a half-dozen humanoid forms haunted the floors and walls of the room. Elizabeth found herself fascinated with them, tracing their progress across the shelves and chandeliers and heavy carpets.

"You okay?" John leaned in to whisper. Elizabeth nodded and pressed her hands in her lap. *Focus*, she reminded herself. She had done so well today, she thought—at least she hoped she had. Just a little while longer. Then she could rest. Then she could grieve.

Annette cleared her throat. "Well," she said. "Thank you all for coming. And thank you, Elizabeth, for hosting us in your home." She coughed again, a little nervously, and Elizabeth tried to give her an encouraging nod. She had always liked Annette. Did Annette like her? She wasn't sure—most likely the woman had never given her a passing thought. That's what her husband always said, that Elizabeth was thinking so much of whether others might approve of her that she forgot whether or not she approved of them! But with Annette, Elizabeth did know. She liked her very much.

Oh, bother! Her mind was wandering again. Annette was now saying something about legal procedures. Elizabeth made her face grow very serious and nodded along when John Jr. did.

Everyone else seemed to be paying a great deal of attention to Annette. Luke, the chef, looked a little green. He had been so odd these past few months, jumpy and with enough nervous energy to sometimes make Elizabeth's head spin. On the far couch sat Michael in between Vanessa and Edward—Michael seemed more annoyed than anything, possibly because his mother kept squeezing his knee and his father kept alternating between resting his chin in his hand, with a petulant, thoughtful look on his face, and leaning back with his eyes narrowed and lips puckered, perhaps preparing for some unsavory surprise. Tatiana was the last guest: she sat completely poised now, unaffected. Elizabeth felt some warmth towards her. Tatiana understood. Tatiana knew what a wonderful man John Sr. was, just what a great loss it had been to their family.

Dear me, Elizabeth thought, as she turned, startled, as Annette pronounced her name. It was beginning!

But Elizabeth couldn't seem to focus. Next to her, John Jr.'s whole body tightened. She watched the blood drain from his face. Elizabeth looked around, watching as Edward's eyes widened, as Vanessa's mouth opened in a little *O*, as Tatiana flushed crimson and Luke leapt up from his chair, eyes wild, shaking his head.

"Oh, my," Elizabeth said out loud. Annette glanced up at her, sympathy in her eyes. That was when Elizabeth knew it was not going well.

CHAPTER 7

*J*ohn was shocked.

He did his best to keep it together for his mother's sake. Even as his stomach churned, even as his head spun, even as his mouth went bone-dry and he thought he might be sick all over the plaid carpet he had sat reading *Treasure Island* on as a boy.

He felt his mother watching him and squeezed her hand. Annette finished reading, looking from Luke to John and his mother and back. She looked horribly uncomfortable.

"I'm sorry," she said to John, hands shaking as she set down the will. "I didn't know until earlier today. He must have —it was changed, obviously."

"Supremely generous!" Edward said, from the sofa. He had lifted himself into a half-crouch, as if ready to pounce on the piece of paper to secure his fortune. John felt like he had entered into some nightmare.

"So fantastically generous," Vanessa said, fanning herself with one hand. Far from her usual languid self, she now seemed alert, even giddy. "A wonderful man, I always said."

Equal shares. That was what the will had revealed. John's father had divided his estate into eight equal portions, after charitable donations and other expenses: portions for Edward, Vanessa, Michael, Luke, Annette, Tatiana, Elizabeth, and himself. John Eastwick Sr.'s wife and child were to share the inheritance equally with their relations and some favored staff.

John's first coherent thoughts were that perhaps this was how it should work—perhaps his father, being the man that he was, wanted to share his wealth with those who shared his blood and his life. Perhaps John, as his son, had no right to feel the gut punch that he did, had no claim on the millions (for millions it was) that had been taken from his hands and distributed among the others. John had never thought before of the size of his father's estate, and to think of it now, being sawed apart and distributed to so many and in such a way.... Perhaps it was greed and malice that made him so queasy.

With an effort, then, he said, "It's fine, Annette. It's what my father wanted, so it's what we want, too."

Annette just stared at him. "You'll have to sell the house," she said finally, lowering her voice as Edward chatted jovially with Vanessa over Michael's head. "The estate itself...your father had a great deal of other funds, but this property is substantial. And if your mother takes over some of his liquid funds..."

John took his mother's hand instinctively, but Elizabeth seemed not to hear the lawyer. Instead she looked over at John, eyes dreamy and unfocused. "It isn't good, dear, is it?" she said.

"We'll manage."

"Of course we will."

Ridiculous, John told himself. Of course they'd manage. His father's death had made him a millionaire, even if he had been given an equal portion as his simpering aunt and snide uncle. Acting like this was a hardship was despicable. John gathered his courage and rose. Luke rose as well and half-stumbled after John as the latter made his way to the kitchen and poured himself a hearty drink.

Luke followed suit.

"I'm so sorry," Luke gushed, after a long swig of whiskey. "I didn't know—I would never, if I had known, I would've told him not to."

"It's fine, Luke."

The chef looked wild. He had always been kind to John, giving him extra portions of desserts and spreading his vegetables thin on the plate when he was younger, so it looked to his parents like he was eating more than he was. Luke had been quiet, almost antisocial, but still a benevolent presence in the house, someone who was so reliable and so regular that it was easy to forget about him, a piece of machinery that was never questioned because it worked so very well.

"I'm glad you're getting a portion," John said, hoping that by saying it enough times, it would be true. And it wasn't just about the money, not entirely—John was hurt, logically or not, by the optics of it: that his father would encourage the reading of a will that showed he placed his wife and only child on the same level as everyone else important in his life. Was that selfishness? John's mind spun: he couldn't think clearly right then, and so couldn't tell.

Luke fussed about in the kitchen while John drank, opening the fridge, putting bottles away in drawers, occasionally letting his eyes slide over to John. He seemed to want to say something else, to be gathering his breath for another sympathetic onslaught, and John, too weary for it, poured himself another hefty dose of whiskey and left the room.

CHAPTER 8

$\mathcal{E}$dward sidled up to Elizabeth, draping one meaty hand around her shoulders. His brother's widow shuddered at the touch; Edward scowled but let the insult pass. It would have been easier to make his request if he had indeed been stiffed in the will, he thought, easier to force himself on Elizabeth's hospitality. Now he had to rely on charm, something Edward Eastwick had always been lacking.

"Dear Elizabeth," he began. "It's near nine o'clock. My wife and I have been so grateful for your hospitality and presence." He coughed. Too formal. "Thank you, my dear. Now, we've both had a few drinks, and I was wondering, that is, I think it might be prudent—"

"We'd like to stay in a spare bedroom tonight," Vanessa said, coming up to Edward's elbow. Elizabeth, still perched on the couch where she had first heard the will read to the rest of the room, looked up at her sister-in-law blandly.

"Stay in a spare bedroom," Elizabeth repeated.

"Yes, Elizabeth. We're in no state to drive. I daresay you should extend the same offer to the rest of your guests."

"Oh, Annette and Luke were always planning to stay the night," Elizabeth said, waving a lazy hand towards where

29

Annette had just left for the kitchen. "Tatiana? Would you like to stay, too? We can make up a bed for you."

The secretary turned pink and looked at the remaining people in the room: Elizabeth, Vanessa, Edward, and Michael. She seemed to be weighing her options.

"Okay," she said, blushing. "If you don't mind."

Edward exchanged a triumphant glance with Vanessa. He had to stop himself from embracing his wife right then and there. It had been a wonderful day, a successful day, a *magnificent* day. Perhaps his luck was finally turning. Perhaps it would all come out right after all—just as it was supposed to.

"Cheer up," Edward said jovially as he clapped his scowling son on the back. Vanessa gathered her purse. "Will be nice to spend a night in the old family home, eh? Good for the soul."

"Aunt Elizabeth," Michael said, "is there any chance I could have, uh, a room a little *apart* from my parents?"

"That seems advisable," Vanessa said, throwing Edward a rare mischievous look. Michael gagged. Even Elizabeth looked scandalized. Tatiana, meanwhile, took the opportunity to beeline for the kitchen.

Oh yes, Edward thought. This was going to be an *excellent* night.

CHAPTER 9

*a*n hour and a half later, John had dragged himself to his room, showered, poured the rest of his drink down the drain, gone to the kitchen to refill his drink on second thought, and finally locked himself back in his room. It was hard to believe that any of this could indeed be real: he felt at any moment that he would go to sleep and wake up with his father there, his father's reputation unscathed, and his father's will only a theoretical, faraway thing that he never had to worry about.

When he went over the evening in his mind, John found he was most troubled by Annette's disquietude. The sharp lawyer had guided his father and his estate for years; why should she be so surprised? Perhaps because the will was vastly different than the one before, though if that were true, John couldn't imagine why. He and his father had had no major falling out. Neither had John's parents. But then, maybe his father intended to be generous, not punitive: after all, it wasn't as though he had cut his son and wife out of the will altogether.

John took a sip of his drink anytime the will entered his head, and so let his thoughts drift syrupy and beige-colored to his past few years at college, now themselves tinged with bitterness. He thought of when he had first gotten his acceptance letter to Montvale, how proud his father had been, how he had shaken John's hand and said, *I always knew it, my boy! You're destined for great things.*

John had believed it at that moment, too.

His father had driven him to college freshman year, had walked up his suitcases and boxes five sets of stairs to the top-floor room in the historic building where John had been placed. They had had chicken masala that night at the restaurant down the road, and John's father had grown serious and told John that college would be a place of pressure and trials, and that John would have to rely on not just his wit, but his integrity, to make it through. It had made John feel very adult to be having such a conversation with his father, though now he blushed to think of it. What if he had asked John Sr., *Why did you bribe my way into Montvale?* What would his father have to say for himself? How could he possibly have explained it all away?

And then there had been the years that had followed: a freshman year where John had received top honors, a finance internship that summer with a well-to-do firm in New York City, a sophomore year where John had won a fellowship to study abroad in Paris in the spring, another summer where John worked with one of his father's clients and received a serious offer to return after graduation. A junior year where John's penultimate project for the economics department won him the class award, and one final summer where John had stayed on campus, working for a world-renowned professor at the business school, who had written John a glowing recommendation for his application that fall.

And now? Now—nothing.

A future that stretched on, formless and endless. He would not be returning to Montvale. Already the script of his time there had been rewritten, no doubt. He was not the star student with the promising future—he was the boy who had gotten in on the weight of his father's money and deception, who had chosen a major popular with athletes, who had traipsed to Paris on the college's dime and who had taken internships from companies connected to his father. Would the college even let him return? John didn't want to find out. He would withdraw. He would abandon his application to the business college. He would remain home, with his father's ghost, trying to find out what he was meant to do with his life, now that all of his previous dreams had proven to be nothing but vapor and smoke.

He wanted nothing more than to dive into his covers, the same ones he had slept under since he was twelve years old, and lose himself in blissful, whiskey-dead sleep. But he felt also that he should check on his mother, that tonight of all nights might be particularly hard for her. As he left his room, John swore he heard a door shutting quickly in the wing, but he could neither see nor hear anyone as he tiptoed over to the master suite.

His mother was still up; she was rubbing cream on her cheeks and smiled at John as her long fingers dabbed light, gentle circles under her eyes.

"John, darling," Elizabeth Eastwick said, motioning to the armchair across from her vanity. "Trouble sleeping?"

"No. Just wanted to say goodnight."

"Goodnight, dear."

A pause, awkward on John's end. He had seen his mother sob multiple times over the past few days; he had gotten good at that particular script. But this one, where the grief weighed between them, mundane and heavy—he wasn't sure how to proceed here. At what point could they ignore the elephant in the room? At what point would the death of John's father cease to be an elephant?

"Do you think he did it?" John blurted out. It wasn't what he had wanted to talk about tonight; it seemed selfish to fuss over it when his mother was still grieving, still trying to process not only the loss of her husband but the loss of her finances. But he couldn't help himself. "Do you think he bribed someone to get me in?"

Elizabeth put down her green tea eye cream and picked up a dainty serum bottle, which she used to pump two drops of milky white liquid into her outstretched hand. "I don't know, darling. I think if he was here, he wouldn't describe it like that."

"Cheated, then. Bent the rules. To get me in."

Elizabeth pursed her lips, rubbing the serum into the fine lines that ran down either side of her nose. "He might have. He wanted the best for you."

"Did you know about it?"

"No." She spun in her chair to face him, her eyes full and sad. "I wish I did, John. I wish I could explain this for you." She reached out and squeezed John's hand. "But we know your father. What a good heart he has. If he made a mistake like this…well, he did it in your best interests."

"That doesn't excuse it." Or the humiliation of it, John thought, though he bit his tongue. "I was taking a spot from someone who deserved it."

"Oh, I don't know if—"

"We can't dance around it, Mom. It was wrong." He felt his temper rising, but mostly because he wanted her to keep fighting with him, keep arguing away the reasons he offered, so that he could somehow really believe that it wasn't so bad, that his father had acted rightly. But Elizabeth only nodded sadly.

"He made a mistake," she said. "But he's not here anymore, so we'll have to forgive him."

"About the will, too?"

"Oh, John."

He watched his mother closely; she looked bone tired,

running one hand across her forehead, long silk sleeves rustling with the motion.

"Did you know he changed the will?" John asked.

"Let's talk about it tomorrow."

"Just tell me, did you know?"

Elizabeth sighed. "No, John."

A thousand questions bubbled up to his lips, along with a surge of rage twice as large as before. "Uncle Edward?" John said. "*Aunt Vanessa?* Do you know Uncle Edward asked me if Montvale had kicked me out yet tonight? He was practically salivating."

"I'm sorry, honey."

And she looked so sad, and tired, and small, that John's rage left just as quickly as it had come. "Don't be sorry," John said, aiming for lightness and ending up with just tired, his voice cracking at the end. "I'm sorry, Mom. It's not—we don't have to talk about it." He hugged her to him, long enough that she wouldn't see his tears.

CHAPTER 10

*E*dward peeled back the duvet on the queen-sized bed and inspected the sheets beneath. "What thread count, do you think?"

Vanessa wrinkled her nose. "How should I know?"

"Do you see a tag? Look on your side."

Vanessa rolled her eyes and unwound the towel from her hair.

Edward fiddled with the sheets a bit more, running his fingers over the soft cream fabric. He wouldn't mind having sheets like this. He wouldn't mind having a house like this. Between him, his wife, and his son, they technically owned more of the Eastwick estate than his brother's widow and son. He spent a few moments dreaming about whether he'd want to keep the large house, or sell it. Money could do so many things…

"Turn out the light, Edward."

He blinked and looked over at the marble lamp on the nightstand. "What time should we do it?"

Vanessa nestled into the thick pillows. "We've had such a good night, Edward. Why complicate it?"

"Well, why not? Good luck breeds good luck."

"And we have more to protect, now," Vanessa said. "Let's sleep on it."

"We won't be staying all together another night."

"So?"

"So. Now is the best opportunity." He smiled—not even his wife's protests could touch his good mood.

"It's a little *pointless* now, isn't it?" she said, propping herself up on one elbow. "I mean, after the will…"

"Oh, my darling, you underestimate these people," Edward said. "What if it's all a lie? A misdirection? Maybe that wasn't the proper will after all."

"If you thought that, you wouldn't be in such a good mood."

"Regardless, it wouldn't hurt to have a little insurance."

He smiled at Vanessa; she stared fish-eyed at him back. Edward was still too jubilant from the evening's strange turn of events to really doubt his fortune, but he was a prudent enough man to not depend on it. And besides, if all shook out as had been promised, would it really be a crime, anyway?

"Fine," Vanessa said. "In an hour. When everyone is in bed."

CHAPTER 11

To John's great surprise, it took him no time at all to fall asleep.

But the world of his dreams was not the idyllic, comforting refuge he had hoped: no, in his dreams he was back at Montvale, in the office of a dean he had never met before, trying without success to explain himself to this blank-faced, disapproving man. His words came slow and jumbled; he did not want to attack his father, did not want to even admit that his father could have done something wrong. "Misunderstanding," he tried to say, but the more he talked, the graver the dean looked, until John found himself babbling about the will and Uncle Edward and how it just wasn't fair.

"Why should the world be fair for cheaters?" the dean had said.

A thump roused John from the nightmare. He rubbed his eyes, rolling over to check the clock. Half past midnight. Too many hours to go until he could pull himself out of bed, until the guests in the house would finally leave him and his mother alone.

He shut his eyes again, but John was now very much awake. He thought about getting more whiskey, or perhaps one of those herbal teas his mother always used to help her fall asleep, when the creak of the floorboards made John go still.

It was a familiar feeling. When John had been a child, he had often struggled to sleep in the large house, imagining first ghosts and then home invaders coming in to snatch him. Now he held himself under the covers, wrinkling his toes to make sure his body was safely inside the bed—no parts hanging over —in service of the old superstition.

Silence held for a few moments longer. Then another long, slow creak. John cocked his head. The noise was only natural, with so many people staying overnight—but why did it sound as though the person did not *wish* to be heard? Surely if they were just striding to the bathroom, or in search of a glass of water, their footsteps would be more confident, or at the very least, more regular. He couldn't imagine someone being *that* concerned about not waking anyone else up.

Unless they were doing something that they did not wish to be seen.

The thought entered his head, ugly and ungracious. But John did not feel particularly gracious that night. He sat up in bed and grabbed a sweatshirt hanging over the back of his desk chair. Then, keeping his footsteps to the quiet floorboards he had learned by heart as a child, John strode to the door and teased it open.

The hallway was empty. John slipped out, but the door betrayed him: as it widened to offer him passage through, it creaked on its old hinges, and John winced. He moved quickly down the hall, in case he could catch anyone wandering... perhaps into rooms they shouldn't be. But if someone had been out here, they were long gone.

Still, John thought he could hear low voices, and moved to the main staircase. They seemed to be coming from the kitchen, along with a dull light that cast an orange glow over the polished hardwood. He listened, half-embarrassed, half-defiant. Shouldn't he know all of the secrets of his own house?

But the voices were too muffled; John would not hear anything unless he walked downstairs, and suddenly a wave of despair and fatigue crashed over him. What would it matter? What would it change if it was Uncle Edward and Aunt Vanessa, gloating over the will? Or Annette talking to his mother, offering sympathy, far-fetched explanations, half-hearted and impossible solutions? Nothing would change what had happened tonight. What had happened days ago, years ago.

He turned to walk back to his room. As he did, though, he noticed one of the doors in the corridor thrown wide open. Perhaps that was where the nighttime wanderer had taken refuge—though the open door seemed a foolish sign. He crept closer, motivated more by a desire to delay the inevitable return to bed than by any true curiosity. He slipped around the other side of the door and peered into the room.

It took a few moments for his eyes to adjust to the stillness. Moonlight filtered in from the long, iron-grated windows, bathing the furniture in pale blue light. He froze, realizing he had walked into a bedroom in use—there, over the armchair near the window, was a woman's dress, and on top of the cracked wooden coffee table, an oversized leather purse. Tatiana's.

He blushed as his eyes skipped neatly over to the bed and away, the figure of the secretary lying across it. She was wearing a full pajama set, probably lent by John's mother, sleeping belly-up on top of the covers. He grabbed the door to shut it behind him, wincing as it creaked, not able to help his eyes from straying back to the secretary to see if she had awoken.

Nothing. She was utterly still.

John began to tug at the door again, gritting his teeth as

the door creaked again. Damn old houses. But the secretary was still.

Too still.

He let go of the door at once. His eyes widened. He felt torn between fleeing entirely and rushing forward to shake Tatiana awake.

"Tatiana!" John shouted. And then, more frightened, "Tatiana!"

CHAPTER 12

*M*ichael was the first to arrive. "John," he said, breathless. "John! What is—"

And then somehow in the jumble they found themselves in front of Tatiana, pressing her wrist, feeling her neck, leaning down in front of her mouth to listen for any sound of breathing. Michael went to fetch a hand mirror and came back, holding it over Tatiana's blue lips as John plucked at his hair and fought his rising panic.

"She's breathing?" John said, hoping fervently that the secretary had passed out, that she had had too much to drink or too many sleeping pills or *anything*. "She's breathing, isn't she? You can see it?"

Michael didn't answer, only held the mirror over Tatiana's mouth for a few moments longer. By now Uncle Edward and Aunt Vanessa had ventured to the door, both in their borrowed pajamas, faces agape. Uncle Edward's looked grotesque, his features almost a mockery of surprise, and John felt a stab of hate towards him.

"Nothing," Michael said. He shuddered and took a quick step back from the body. "Someone call 9-1-1."

Aunt Vanessa gave a little mew of fear and stepped back.

Seconds later, Annette appeared, grim and sober, and not long after, Luke behind her. The large chef balked when he saw Tatiana and blanched when Aunt Vanessa pushed past him with a miserable, "I think I'm going to be sick."

John stumbled back. "I'll get my phone," he said. Any excuse to be out of that room. He fancied he could smell death on Tatiana, the decay already at work in her body, though of course that was impossible. He slid past Annette, who grabbed his arm and squeezed, eyes wide. If Annette was worried, he thought, things were bad.

He stumbled down the hallway, mind whizzing. Call 9-1-1. A body. A body in the house.

Murder.

The word made him shudder. It couldn't be true. Death had come to Eastwick already—certainly they'd be spared another tragedy such as this. Unless some horrible door had opened, and now tragedy after tragedy would follow, chipping away at the estate of Eastwick, at the family of John Eastwick Sr. until nothing was left.

He retrieved his phone from his room and dialed the three numbers, feeling all the while that it was some sort of colossal mistake, a part of him even feeling guilty for wasting the police's time. He strode back to Tatiana's room as he described the situation to the first responder: a woman, not breathing, in her bed.

"Should we do CPR?" John said, electricity rushing through him. Why hadn't he thought of it before? For heaven's sake, what had they been thinking? "Should we start it now? Do we need two people?" Michael, Annette, and Luke were outside the room waiting; the door was shut, and Michael blocked it when John tried to go in, gently taking his cousin by the shoulder. The first responder was saying something, but John's ears were buzzing.

"Why don't you sit down?" Michael said kindly.

"CPR," John said, and promptly passed out.

CHAPTER 13

The next hour was a mad flurry of activity. The ambulance came; the medics entered the room, efficient and cold, and returned minutes later to talk to the police. They did not move Tatiana.

The police officers had each of the guests of the house sit in a separate room to wait for an interview. John had first to find his mother: he had not seen her in all of the chaos, though she was the first person he thought of when he came to, shaken awake by Michael after his embarrassing fainting spell. Annette clung close to John's side as he checked his mother's room, and then the master bathroom and the kitchen in search of her. The lawyer whispered to him as his panic rose, as he went from walking to running to sprinting through the house, calling out his mother's name even after the police had arrived and given their instructions.

He found her finally back in the master, when he checked the balcony. She was sitting in the cool night air with her legs drawn up to her chest, shivering in a heavy navy robe. The lights from the police cars glowed red and blue on her skin as John embraced her. "What are you doing out here?" he said. "Don't you see what's happening?"

"Oh," Elizabeth said, catching John's hand and squeezing. "Oh, John, it's like it's cursed."

"What is? Mom, come inside, please. It's cold."

"This house. This family. This town." Elizabeth shuddered, drawing her robe closer to herself. John felt another wave of fear rise in his chest and forced it down. Why hadn't his mother come in when he had first discovered Tatiana's body? Hadn't she heard him crying out for her in the ensuing minutes? Why hadn't the police cars finally roused her from her trance and invited her to go inside? More creeping doubts entered his mind, ugly doubts, and John thrust them away.

"Come inside, Mom. Nothing's haunted."

She obeyed, though they both knew that it wasn't true. The town, St. Clair, was decidedly so. It was a point of pride, even, for the townspeople. It made them feel special—that they weren't just another wealthy lakeside suburb, that there was something mystical, *powerful*, about them. St. Clair had more than its fair share of strange sightings, ghost stories, and local folklore—more, the crimes that occurred within its borders seemed to slip and slide off of its citizens' consciousnesses, to evaporate into the air. A horrific murder might be forgotten decades, years, or even months after, as if the town itself was erasing the act. John just wished the same power of erasure could take back the events of that night.

John got his mother safely to an armchair in the master bedroom, one with a green and white plaid blanket slung over the back. John pulled it off and wrapped it around his mother's frail shoulders, trying not to think about how much older she looked in that moment, shoulders bent, face drawn. Fear stabbed through him: what if he should lose her, too? What if the world *was* cursed, and the death of John's father portended some awful destruction of all the rest of his life?

John squeezed his eyes shut and took a breath. His mother looked up at him and squeezed his hand.

"It will all be okay, darling," she said.

"Tatiana is dead."

His mother did not flinch. She did not even look surprised. John's stomach turned over. "Is that so," she said slowly. "Tatiana."

"She might have been murdered."

"Murdered? Says who?"

"I don't know. The police are here. They're not moving her. And they want to question us all, one by one."

"Starting now, please," a voice from the door said, and John jumped. He had thought he would have a minute longer with his mother. A minute more to assess her, to warn her, to protect her. He glanced at the police officer, a serious young woman with dark brown eyes and her hair pulled back in a braid. At her pointed look, he put away any thoughts of asking to talk to his mother in private for a few moments more.

"Should we call a lawyer?" he asked his mother, taking a few steps towards the door.

"A lawyer?"

"Do you need a lawyer, Mr. Eastwick?" the police officer said. For a moment, John expected his father to answer her.

"No, I don't," John said, recovering. "But my mother's grieving. I don't think you should question her without—"

"Annette's here, darling. She'll come sit with me, if you're worried."

The police officer was staring at John now. What was her name? Detective Stone? She certainly looked as harsh and as unrelenting as one as she assessed him, and heat rose to his face. He knew he was acting guilty. But he wouldn't lose his mother, too, on the off chance she had anything at all to do with it. Not that she did. Not that Tatiana *had* been murdered. It was just his mind, this memorial service, the awful suddenness of his father's death...suddenly everything felt sinister, oppressive, dangerous.

"Can she do that?" John asked the detective. "Wait until Annette is with her—Annette Jenkins?"

"Entirely up to your mother," the detective said. "Come with me, please."

She directed him into one of the many guest rooms of the mansion; strange, thought John, how now the house seemed to belong entirely to the police officers and no longer to his family. The guest room was one of the unused ones facing the back of the house. John supposed they were searching the others.

Not long after, a thin, wiry man with ebony skin and a confident gait walked into the room and shut the door. "Detective Bordeaux," he said, extending one hand. "I'm afraid this might be a long night for you."

CHAPTER 14

"*H*orrifying," Annette said, pacing up and down the ballroom where the memorial service had just been held. The police officer watched her, notepad at the ready, blue eyes steady on her. Annette bit at a cuticle and wondered why she was even talking. Why she felt so strange, so giddy, so *unhinged*. Murder. What an ugly word. What a horrid concept!

And yet sometimes people had good motivations for the terrible things that they did.

"I suppose I should call a lawyer," Annette said, with a nervous laugh.

"Would you like one?" the officer said, leaning forward on his chair, pen poised in one freckled hand. Despite being a lawyer herself, Annette had next to no experience with cops. That wasn't her kind of law. She didn't know how to behave. She didn't know if even now, the cop watching her pace the room had decided she was guilty.

"Well, maybe I do," Annette. "Not now, I guess. Maybe later?"

The cop didn't answer her question.

"Go ahead, ask me," Annette said. The silence was worse

49

than anything, and she continued to pace, quickening her stride. She wondered what Luke was saying, if she should have warned him to get a lawyer himself.

"Where were you between ten p.m. and midnight?"

"Is that when the murder took place?" Annette blurted. "Oh! I suppose you won't tell me. Routine questions, and the like. Well, I was in the kitchen. With Luke."

"And what were you two doing in the kitchen?"

Annette's throat was dry. She massaged it, wondering if she could ask for water. Would asking make her seem guilty, like she was choking on words that were nothing more than lies? "Just talking."

"So late at night?" the officer said.

Annette settled for coughing to clear her throat. "We had a lot to discuss," Annette said. "We've both been with the family for a long while. Horrible, what happened to Mr. Eastwick."

"What time did you two arrive down in the kitchen?"

"Ten-thirty? Eleven? I can't remember."

"Start from the beginning then, please. You went upstairs after the memorial service…"

"And the reading of the will. After that."

At the officer's blank expression, Annette sighed. She explained, briefly, the shock that had come over all of them at the reading. Her own embarrassment and uncertainty at what to do right after. They had all been tired, shocked, tentative with one another. Annette's head had hurt to think of the legal circus that might ensue if someone contested the will, and had wracked her brain for a good estate attorney to refer Elizabeth to. John Eastwick Jr. had shown Annette to her room. She had showered and collapsed into bed, but her thoughts had continued to race, and eventually she had texted Luke and asked him to meet her for a coffee in the kitchen.

"And what time was that?"

Annette pulled out her phone. "10:34. He responded at 10:38, and we were both down there, oh, a few minutes after."

"Luke will confirm those times, too?"

"They're on his phone as well," Annette said, and then snapped her mouth shut, in case her words had come out too tersely. "I'm sure he will?"

The officer said nothing, just looked at Annette with that inscrutable expression. Perhaps, then, Luke had already said much more than he should have. Perhaps he had given it all away, panicking under pressure. *It doesn't matter*, Annette told herself. She couldn't understand why she cared so much, why the thought of it made sweat prick at the nape of her neck, behind her ears, down the small of her back. *Not yet not yet not yet*, she begged in silent prayer.

"And how long did you remain down there talking?"

"Until we heard John shouting. By the time we were up there, everyone was in the room already—Edward, Vanessa, Michael. And Tatiana—Tatiana was, well, dead. She is dead, isn't she?"

"What did you and Luke talk about in the kitchen?" the police officer said.

"Is that important?"

"It might be."

"Well, like I said. We just wanted to talk over everything. The memorial service, the will…it was all so horrid."

"Is that what Luke will say, too?"

Annette heard the implicit threat in the question. She had used similar techniques herself in the past, in service of her clients. But now she couldn't think straight, couldn't muster a sufficiently dismissive response that would prove how little she had to fear and release her from the tight hold of the detective's questions. "Yes?" she said, her voice squeaking. Wouldn't he? Would he at the very least know to keep his mouth shut?

The police officer held her gaze for a few more beats. "All right," he said. Meaning what? Meaning, *I know you're lying but*

51

I'll confront you later about it, when my net's tighter? "Until 10:34, what were you doing?"

"Washing up for bed."

"You went up around ten o'clock. And showered for thirty-four minutes? Did you do anything else?"

"Moisturized, brushed my teeth. Considered flossing and didn't."

"All of that took you thirty-four minutes?"

"I'm surprised it didn't take me much longer."

"Did you walk past Tatiana's room on your way down to the kitchen?"

"No, it was in the other wing of the house."

"And if someone were to spot you in that wing, Tatiana's wing, around 10:20 p.m. that night, what would you say?"

Annette's heart skipped a beat. "But I wasn't."

"Are you sure? Perhaps you were going to the bathroom?"

Snake, thought Annette. He didn't want to offer her an excuse; he wanted to lure her into a trap, get her to say that she had lied to him. "I never went to that wing," Annette said. "Who said they saw me there?"

"Perhaps no one," said the officer. Annette's heart picked up, drowning out her thoughts with its steady thrum.

CHAPTER 15

"*I* don't understand why I can't be with my husband," Vanessa said. They had taken her to the basement, a refurbished spot with fairy lights and dark oak and black stools, with a home theater on one end and a pool table on the other. Vanessa always thought that such basements were trashy, like trying to recreate a bar within the bowels of one's home. *She* would never waste such money and space. If Vanessa got her hands on the Eastwick estate, she would restore it to the class it deserved. Or rather, tell a designer her vision (maybe Vicki? Or Joanne, quite possibly Joanne from yoga) and pay them enough money to finish the work and not bother her about it until it was done. Oh, that sounded nice!

"We're just going to ask you both a few questions," the officer said, his double chin quivering with the words. Vanessa crossed her arms and swiveled back and forth on the black stool. The male officer looked young and earnest; Vanessa had little respect for either. She tapped her foot impatiently to show that she did not appreciate her time being wasted.

"Why can't you ask me together with him?" Vanessa pushed. "Isn't that spousal privilege?"

"Not quite. Now, can you walk me through where you were after the memorial service? And the reading of the will?"

Vanessa sighed. "Edward was rather tired, so we had Elizabeth show us to a room. We went straight to bed, after I showered."

"And what time was that?"

"Oh, I don't know. 10:30? I had some melatonin and I was out—well, for a little while, anyway, before all the racket."

"Describe what you heard, please."

"I don't know." Vanessa pursed her lips. "I thought I was dreaming at first. People shouting. Someone screamed, maybe? I don't remember. And then I was throwing my robe on. I thought perhaps something had happened to Michael— mother's instincts, you know. Edward followed me out and we ran until we came to that poor woman's room. She was dead already, I think. Michael and John were trying to save her, but they couldn't."

"Trying to save her how?"

"Checking her pulse, that sort of thing. I think Michael might have been able to do something if John hadn't been in the way, but of course John couldn't help himself. Kept jumping in. And all that shouting!"

"How did Ms. Orlov look to you then?"

Vanessa blinked. "Dead. Blonde. Is that what you mean?"

The detective gave her a strange look. "Did you see anyone else in between when you went to bed and arrived at Tatiana's room? Or hear anything as you were falling asleep?"

"Well, Elizabeth, but I didn't think much of that."

"You saw Elizabeth when?" the detective said, his voice sharpening.

Vanessa examined her nails. "When we were on the way to Tatiana's room. She was walking towards the kitchen—I just assumed she wanted a cup of tea, or something. She was like that in college, never a good sleeper. I came out of my room once and there she was in the common room, reading a book and eating cookies by the sleeve at 3 a.m. It was absolutely ridiculous—of course, then I knew that she had to keep her figure in some clandestine way, as she obviously wasn't *dieting*." Vanessa pronounced the word as if it were a crucial life practice.

"And did you see Elizabeth after that? When you came out of Tatiana's room?"

"I never said I was in Tatiana's room," Vanessa snapped. "I was standing at the threshold with my husband. Ask Michael or John. They'll tell you."

"Of course. But Elizabeth—?"

"I didn't see her again. I was a bit distracted by the dead body."

"Did your husband see her?"

"Well, we could ask him, if you'd let us answer your questions together."

The detective gave her a bland smile.

"Oh, and Luke," Vanessa added, stroking her chin with one finger. "Luke, too. Just the once, when I was leaving the bathroom earlier in the night. He was going down the hallway to his room, and he had a drink in his hand. A mug, I think."

"Luke was staying in the wing where Tatiana was?"

"Was he? If you say so."

The detective pressed her more on this, asking at about what time she saw Luke (10:30, or thereabouts, but she wasn't paying attention), whether he was alone (to the best of her knowledge, yes), whether he had gone into Tatiana's room (if that had been the case, their job would be pretty easy, wouldn't it?). Soon the detective seemed to realize that he would get little else from this line of questioning; he switched tactics.

"How well did you know Tatiana Orlov?" he asked.

Vanessa was playing with the drink coasters set neatly in a wooden case at the edge of the bar. They had a fake coat of arms (tacky) and the name *Eastwick* done up in medieval-looking letters on the bottom. How horrid. She'd get rid of those immediately, replace them with crystal coasters from that shop at the lake's edge where the mayor's wife reportedly did all of her home shopping—snagging a feature in *Lakeside Living* last fall.

"Not in the least," Vanessa said, sniffing. "She was a secretary, wasn't she?"

"She was. And yet, close enough to your brother-in-law to be invited to the reading of his will."

"That should tell you something," Vanessa said. She didn't feel bad about it one bit. The way Elizabeth was always walking around, acting like she was better than Vanessa just because she had married the richer brother, when Vanessa was the one who had introduced them in the first place, when really, looking back at their college days, it was *Vanessa* who had spoken to John Eastwick Sr. first, but then Edward had come into the room, Edward with his stupid grin and his flashing gold wristwatch, and he had told her she was the most beautiful woman at the party. Sometimes she wondered afterwards if he had only spoken to her to drive the knife into his brother. Sometimes she wondered what would have happened if she had stayed talking to John, if she had ended up with him. Vanessa had not had a bad life; she understood that. But it was always a life of shadow, of comparison, of being *less than* simply because she had married the younger, less ambitious, less wealthy brother, and every Christmas and Easter had to visit the elder and see what their lives might have been if either of them had made more of them.

"What are you implying about Mr. Eastwick's secretary?" the officer said, pulling Vanessa out of her reverie.

"Hmm?" Vanessa said. "Oh, nothing. I don't know anything. But I suppose you'll want to ask Elizabeth about that."

"I understand that Ms. Orlov was to have received an equal share in Mr. Eastwick's estate?"

"Yes." Vanessa felt a stab of jealousy before she remembered that, of course, Tatiana was dead. Would the portion go to Tatiana's descendants? Or would it be theirs to redistribute among the seven of them now, instead of eight? She would ask as soon as she could—as soon as it might not seem suspicious.

"Did that surprise you?"

"Of course."

"You thought that the money would go only to family?"

"Only to *immediate* family," Vanessa said, sniffing. "That's how John was. Stingy. Tight-fisted. Always thinking of his wife and son first."

"How horrible," the officer muttered, and Vanessa loudly agreed. "So why do you think that the three of you were included in the will, then? You, your husband, and your son."

"I think he probably had some sort of mental breakdown," Vanessa said. "Stress, maybe? That's the only thing that makes sense. Maybe he knew this college scandal would come out, and he panicked. You've heard of that, of course?" The detective nodded. "Right. So maybe John knew that his reputation was about to be shredded, and, and he thought—well, he'd just divide the estate up a different way."

"And any idea why he'd do that?"

"The scandal," Vanessa said, pouting. She had connected the two thoughts loosely; wasn't it the detective's job to fill in the gaps? "I don't know. Ask his wife."

The detective spoke with her a few more minutes; Vanessa grew increasingly petulant and increasingly tired. She didn't like all this death business. It had been exciting at first, but now it was tiresome, and she felt like she couldn't breathe deeply in the same room as the detective. She didn't like the way he looked at her, with those wide and penetrating eyes. She didn't like the way his head had tipped back, just a little bit, at her very first lie.

CHAPTER 16

$\mathcal{E}$lizabeth leaned back in her armchair, wrapping herself again in the blanket that John had used to tuck her in. She felt very much like a child, in fact: tired, confused, dazed, and a little too willing to latch onto the nearest authority to tell her how to behave, to tell her what to do. There was something comforting about having police officers running up and down her house. They were commanding, sure of themselves. They gave her directions and didn't apologize about it, and they didn't offer condolences about her husband. If only the detective in front of her now would stop asking her questions; then, she thought, she might pass a good night's sleep as the police worked away.

"You didn't see or hear anything?" the police officer asked, for the fifth time. Elizabeth could hear the note of annoyance that had crept into his voice.

"No," Elizabeth whispered. She ran through her story again: leaving the library after the reading of the will, double-checking the locks on the front door, running by her husband's old office, by habit, to check that he hadn't left any glasses or mugs for the day. Going up to bed and slipping into her robe, and then taking a short walk through the house again, because sleep seemed much too far away. No, she hadn't seen anyone. She had heard some whispers, maybe, but she couldn't recall where, or about what. Maybe she hadn't heard them after all. And then she had returned to her balcony, to gaze over the grounds and imagine how it all could have gone differently, if only John Sr. hadn't died and left her all alone.

"The house is cursed," Elizabeth told the police officer. "Two deaths in as many weeks."

"I thought you said your husband died at the hospital?"

"Well, that's where he was *declared* dead." Elizabeth shrugged, trying at the same moment to dispel the image that flitted into her head: tubes, bags, metal pipes, plastic lines. Hospital gowns with little anchors and seashells as their patterns, and nurses who spoke to her non-responding husband like he was a child, like he had never run a company or raised a son or started a charity for Alaskan malamutes after their own, Big Dog (named by John Jr. when he was only four), passed away.

The detective was asking now about Tatiana. Elizabeth let her arm drop to one of the chair's sides. She knew she was supposed to look interested, that it was important she seem engaged in these questions in particular. It was not the first time someone had pointed out to her that Tatiana Orlov was a very pretty young woman. Barbara from church had always offered not-so-veiled hints that Elizabeth should keep an eye on her, that in fact, if Barbara were in Elizabeth's shoes, she'd demand her husband change secretaries then and there. But Elizabeth had never minded—Tatiana was good at her job, John Sr. said, and Tatiana had always been kind to her. And Elizabeth had always thought their marriage was so strong, stronger than anyone's. The idea that John Sr. would cheat on her seemed laughable—he was too honest, too ethical, too straight-edged. She had learned her lesson about doubting that long ago.

And yet how could she tell the police officer this? He

would laugh in her face and remind her that her husband was not any of those things. He'd point to Montvale, and that stupid donation that was not a donation, and remind her again of the pain in John Jr.'s face when he had come home, never to return to Montvale again.

No, she could say none of those things. But she could and did tell the police officer that she did not know Tatiana very well, that her husband had been fond of the girl, that she hadn't noticed anything illicit between them, that she did think it odd that Tatiana was included in the will.

"Though, to be honest, I'm surprised that anyone else was," Elizabeth said. "Besides John Jr. and myself. At least, in equal portions."

The police officer wanted to know about this, too. Was the senior Mr. Eastwick especially fond of Luke, Annette, and Tatiana? Did he always have some plan to compensate them in his will, even for a lesser amount? When had Mr. Eastwick made this last-minute change—and hadn't he consulted his wife? Surely Elizabeth had signed something.

Here Elizabeth blushed. She was not one of those wives who refused to sign anything her husband put before her. She *trusted* John Sr. It was easier to let him tell her what she needed to sign and be done with it. He would do the same for her. It might sound foolish in retrospect (it always did), but then, if she could not trust her spouse, who could she trust? "I might have signed something," Elizabeth said sheepishly. "I can't remember."

If she had paid more attention, would she have noticed what her husband had done? Would she have asked him if something was going on, if there was a reason he was making the others equal inheritors of his estate? Would she have picked up on Tatiana specifically? Would John Sr. have looked uncomfortable at the question, a little guilty? Would she have known then, with a stab to her stomach that would mean that nothing would ever be the same?

"And your brother-in-law," the police officer said. "Were you surprised that he and his family were included equally?"

"Is that relevant?"

"It might be."

Elizabeth sighed. What if she told him that they were all great friends, that their families had been close for years? She supposed it was only a matter of time. "I was very surprised," she said. "We barely even spoke to them. Edward and John were...estranged."

"The two brothers, you mean?"

"Yes."

"What about you and your sister-in-law? Or the two boys?"

"Michael and John Jr.? I think they like each other well enough. Vanessa and I used to be friends. When our husbands stopped speaking, though...well, we fell off, too. I haven't seen her in years. The last time was at a Christmas back when their great-aunt was still alive."

"And why were the brothers estranged?"

Elizabeth blinked at him. It seemed so presumptuous, that just because someone had been murdered they could walk around asking about all of her secrets and examining all the dark corners of her life. "They just didn't get along."

"Always? Or did something happen between them?"

Elizabeth shrugged. She thought back to college, when Vanessa had been loud and flirtatious and smooth. When John Sr. (then just John) had been a blushing, awkward young man, too tall to know what to do with most of his limbs. When the four of them had gone out on a double-date, and John and Elizabeth had bonded over how stuffy Edward and Vanessa had been, correcting the waiter on his French pronunciation and making offhand comments about how the seafood on the Spanish coast was greatly superior, even though Elizabeth knew for a fact Vanessa, at least, had never been. They had laughed so hard that night, holding each other's arms.

"We always got along. In the past few years it's been…
more difficult. There was a bit of an altercation."

"Physical?"

"No, not exactly. I don't know what happened. It was at
Christmas."

"At the great-aunt's?"

"Yes."

"What did you see?"

"Nothing. John just came downstairs, flustered. He
wouldn't tell me what was wrong. On the drive home he said,
'That's it, we're done with them.' Or something like that."

"You didn't ask why?"

She didn't need to. She had seen over the years how
condescending Edward could be, how callous and cruel. She
saw the way that jealousy made a monster of him, the more so
as Edward never made much of his life, how he had to hold
on to his first gifts of privilege to maintain even the semblance
of wealth. He and Vanessa had lavished money on trips and
clothes in their early years, which might have been fine if they
had, at the same time, been building careers. But Edward had
started law school, quit law school, entered business school,
quit business school, and finally taken a job at his father's
company that he held on to by the skin of his teeth, always
complaining about the hours and the work when it was really
only charity, John Sr. said, that kept his younger brother
employed. That night, John Sr. had just had his fill.

"I assume they just argued," Elizabeth said, at a loss how
to explain the brothers' long history. "And that was that."

The police officer let the silence unspool between them,
perhaps hoping to tempt Elizabeth to speak more. She folded
her hands over her lap and watched him. He looked down at
his papers, fiddling with them a bit, and cleared his throat.

"Did your brother-in-law have any issues with Ms. Orlov?
Or did anyone else, on that side of the family?"

"I don't see how. Tatiana's been with Mr. Eastwick for, oh,

eight years or so? And she's probably met Edward and the rest a handful of times at most, at Christmas parties. And not for many years."

"She spent more time with your husband?"

"Naturally, since she was his secretary."

"They traveled together?"

"Yes." Elizabeth bristled.

"Helped him with personal things sometimes? Dry cleaning and the like?"

"No. John kept very strict lines about that."

"Are you sure? She didn't, for instance, help out your son with his college application?"

Elizabeth blushed. "No, certainly not. She had nothing to do with that."

"You're sure? But you didn't know your husband had… helped, right?"

"I can't account for everything my husband does." The blood rushed to her face, and Elizabeth felt hot and a little dizzy.

"Did your son think that perhaps she might have known? Or helped?"

"If you're suggesting he killed her because he wanted to keep her quiet, you're dead wrong," Elizabeth said, wincing at her choice of words. "First, John Jr. would never do something like that. Second, the news was already out. And third, if you're looking for a motive, all of us have one—there's a thirty-day survivorship requirement on the will. If you don't survive my husband by thirty days, you don't get your portion of the estate."

"You heard that tonight?"

"Yes."

"It stuck out to you?"

"I didn't remember it being there before, so yes. It stuck out to me."

"I see," the police officer said, and Elizabeth blushed

deeper still. She had, perhaps, been the only one foolish enough to mention it that night. Perhaps she had even been the only one to have noticed it during the reading, to have turned it over in her mind, considering, wondering, musing.

Elizabeth shuddered.

CHAPTER 17

"Oh, ho, ho!" said Edward, tugging at the corner of his dark mustache. "You might think that, but you don't know my brother the way I do."

He was quite enjoying the interrogation, actually, resting on one of the divans in the living room. The detective who was questioning him was a young woman with big brown eyes and a well-cut figure, and she seemed quite suitably impressed to be in the presence of a man like himself. He could tell by the way she nodded her head every time he spoke, the way she deferred to him if they started speaking at the same time, the way her eyes shone every time he said her name. Huzzah! He had his confidence back, and it had only taken one-eighth of his dead brother's estate.

Well, one-seventh, now.

"I never had the pleasure of meeting him," the detective said. "I've only heard good things, of course."

"Excepting the recent news, mmm? Oh, don't act like you don't know—everyone does, by now. The college scandal? Bribing to get John Jr. into school? Never had to do that with my boy, Michael. Smart as a whip. Going places. Never needed a handout from me, though I could have made a few phone calls. Legally, of course."

"Of course. But your brother, you were saying his reputation might not be quite what it seemed—?"

"Trust me, the college is just the tip of it. He was always pushing the lines. Acted like he was this golden child, never did wrong—I saw it, though. I was never fooled!"

The detective nodded. Gullible, that's what she was. He could probably tell her that his brother had murdered a man ten years ago and she would go on scribbling, bright-eyed and earnest. That was the problem with government workers—they weren't paid enough, so the talent level was always mediocre at best.

She had already walked him through where he had been that evening and didn't seem particularly interested in questioning the details he had given her, methodically, carefully, aware that in television shows, at least, detectives analyzed the movements down to the minute. But she had just nodded when he explained he and his wife had gone to bed, and then had started up when they heard John's shouts. She had taken him at his word that he hadn't seen anyone on that trek down the hall, hadn't tried to misdirect him with any leading questions, hadn't even challenged him on a detail to see how he reacted. All of this Edward had been prepared for and been disappointed.

No, the detective just wanted to talk about John, John, dead John. So be it! Just like the old bastard—a young, beautiful woman is murdered in his home, and people still can't stop obsessing about him.

"What was the relationship between Ms. Orlov and your brother?" the detective asked.

"Simple. He was sleeping with her."

A slight pause at that. Edward grinned; he had surprised her. "Really," the detective said. "He told you that?"

"Oh, he didn't have to. A blind man could see it. She was always traveling with him. Came to a few family parties. Elizabeth never liked her—women always get jealous of the younger ones, am I right?" The detective only blinked at him. "And you could tell, this Tatiana, she had that swagger about her."

"Swagger."

"You know." Edward nodded. "Like she had something over on him. Smug. Bragged to Michael once that she was earning six figures already. Wonder why."

"So you and your family knew her a bit, as well?"

"Saw her when my brother John had the balls to bring her around. At family events and the like. Not for a few years, not since John and I fell out."

"I see. And—"

"Makes sense, doesn't it?" Edward said. "Why he gave some money to Annette and Luke. Couldn't make it too obvious he was having an affair with his secretary, right? So slip a few other long-time employees some money, make it seem like he's just a generous fellow when he's the worst kind of scoundrel. John was always clever, I'll give him that."

"Did he ever confirm he was having an affair?"

"No. But we hadn't spoken in years. In fact, come to think of it, that's probably why he included us in the will, too. Didn't have a change of heart or anything—just wanted to cover his tracks some more. Not make it too obvious he was paying off his mistress."

"Seems an odd way to pay her off—to leave her something in the will."

"Young women are nasty," Edward said. "If they don't get their way—woman scorned, and all that. John knew what was good for him. She probably asked, and he delivered. You know she had an Eastwick diamond, don't you?"

"A what?"

"Eastwick diamond. Family tradition. You give the woman you're going to marry—or your mistress, I guess—a diamond ring. Promise ring before the engagement one. Always useful when you need to buy yourself some time." He winked at the detective, but she seemed a little slow—didn't get the joke, didn't react to it. "Anyway, I saw her wearing one on her middle finger, once. Right hand. She covered it when I asked her about it, and when I saw her again, it was off. Couldn't have acted any more suspicious."

"That is interesting. And you're sure it was—an Eastwick diamond, you said?"

"Well, a ring, at any rate. Didn't get a good look. So you see," Edward said, "John's not as innocent as he likes to pretend he is. That's what he always did—act like a good guy, let people think the best of him, when he really wasn't better than anyone else. He was worse. A hypocrite."

"Is that why you two had a falling out?"

Edward blushed. Really, he thought, he didn't need to get into that story then and there. It had nothing to do with anything, and The Incident, as Vanessa had termed it, was years in the past now. And Edward had paid for the dental work.

"One of the many reasons," Edward said. He yawned and stretched. He'd had enough of the questioning for tonight, he thought. He wanted to go back to bed. He wanted to glory in the fact that the past two weeks had been the best in his life, in the fact that he and his family were now rich, his older brother was gone, and most importantly, his brother's reputation was tarnished.

Edward had been proven right after all.

"And if you ask me," Edward said gravely, "you want to know who offed Tatiana?"

"We don't yet know if it's a homicide."

"Right, sure," Edward said. "But when you do, you know who probably got her? Just think about the people who would have the most to lose. Who wouldn't want the affair to come out."

"You mean John's wife and son?"

Edward tapped his temple. "Nothing gets by you, eh? Smart cookie."

The detective smiled blandly at him.

CHAPTER 18

"*Y*ou don't have to be nervous. We have to ask everyone these questions."

The detective was looking kindly at him, but Luke couldn't stop shaking. "I don't know anything," he said again.

The detective flicked his pen and kept one eye on Luke. Luke was disappointing him, he could tell. A wave of shame washed over him. He was disappointing everyone, it seemed. He couldn't help it. And when Mrs. Eastwick found out…

He blushed a deeper red. Didn't he deserve to be happy, too? Why shouldn't he be? He had worked so hard, for so long…why did it have to go this way?

Annette was worried, too. She had been shaken up the whole night. She had told Luke not to say anything without a lawyer present, but had given him a look of warning when he asked if she could be that lawyer.

He needed to get a hold of himself. He needed to be braver. If not for his sake, for hers.

"Keep going," Luke said. "I'm ready."

His voice only shook a little.

CHAPTER 19

*M*ichael crossed his arms over himself and shuddered. The draft from the bay window bit into him, slicing into every open pore. The detective had questioned him only briefly before being called away; maybe they had found another clue. Maybe Tatiana was okay after all.

He wanted to see his parents. More than anything, he felt strongly that he needed to speak to them, to read in their faces what they were thinking and feeling. That would calm him down, he thought. That would slow the out-of-control spinning sensation in his stomach.

"How well did you and your family know Tatiana?" the detective had asked him. But why? Routine, of course it had to be routine, but Michael's thoughts were leaping to the most wild conclusions, the most heart-wrenching speculations. *Not at all*, Michael had replied. They hadn't all been together in one place since what, three years ago? Not since his father and his Uncle John had had that awful row.

The detective had asked about the relationship between his Uncle John and Tatiana, too, and the way that he did made Michael think they suspected something sinister—an affair, or a lawsuit, or something unsavory. Was that even possible? No, it couldn't be. His Uncle John wasn't...Tatiana surely hadn't...Michael pressed the heels of his hands to his eyes.

He was sequestered in the parlor, facing the front driveway of the house, in a room full of whites and grays and black-checkered fabrics. When he looked out the window, he could see the curve of the long gravel drive, circling at the top around a stone fountain and then slithering off into the distance, the opening to the street too far to see. This, Michael thought, was how the truly rich lived: not in the cramped ranch house that his parents had "retired" to, with their leased cars and scraped investment accounts and constant moving of assets. He never talked money with his parents, not directly, but over the years he had seen that their pompous talk about their circumstances was just that, talk. Uncle John, on the other hand, never talked of his wealth, because it was so readily apparent. Michael wouldn't have been surprised to find, indeed, that his parents were months from some sort of real trouble.

He ran a hand through his hair. Not anymore. Now all of them would be well off. An eighth, now a seventh, of Uncle John's fortune! Enough to change each and every one of their lives.

Was it right to still feel a strange twist of hope when he thought about the money, even though Tatiana was dead? When he thought of it, the future stretched out before him, welcoming and bright. His student loans became negligible little gnats. His future job prospects seemed rosy and glowing, nice-to-haves rather than must-haves. His relationship with his family became easy and unforced—his parents would no longer obsess over which vacation they had to miss, which new role his father would try to apply for. They'd all live in luxury. They'd be happy, content, all together.

But would they?

Michael was not young anymore; he knew what greed could do to people. It was just as possible that the money would corrupt. It might have already.

The detective returned, whistling. He gave Michael a nod and sat on the couch next to him with a sigh.

"Quite the family you have here," the detective said. "Must make for some fun family reunions."

Michael did not deign to reply.

They went over again Michael's movements for the night: the memorial service, bed, and then shooting up and sprinting down the hall when he heard his cousin John crying out. He had seen no one. Noticed nothing suspicious.

"John was the first one to see Tatiana," the detective said. "Do you know what the relationship was like between the two of them?"

"She was his father's secretary."

"Anything else?"

Michael forced himself not to roll his eyes. "John's a good kid," he said. "He stays out of trouble. Colors within the lines. No way he'd have become friends with someone who worked for his dad. Isn't even on his radar."

"Why not?"

"It's how his mind works. He puts people in boxes, and they stay there." Michael had firsthand experience of this. It was why Michael was "other" to John, just because he had Edward and Vanessa for parents. Michael couldn't blame him. In some ways, they were destined to never become friends: Michael was three years older, for one, an important fact when they were children. And by the time they were old enough to understand each other, they were old enough to understand the rift between their fathers.

"Was it possible he might have overstepped that boundary at some point?" the detective asked. So earnest. As if just inviting Michael to say that, why yes, John could sometimes be very suspicious.

"Never," Michael said. John, he thought, didn't have a secret in his soul. He wasn't a liar or a fraud or a cheat.

He had never had to be to survive.

CHAPTER 20

*S*omehow, at some point early in the morning, the guests of the Eastwick mansion floated back to their rooms and managed to catch a few hours of fitful sleep. The morning sun burst bright and clear onto the house, outlining blinds in searing red and baking the bedrooms.

John was the first to emerge; he found two of the police detectives had not yet left, though they loudly and cheerily informed him that the body had been moved and then motioned him over.

"Want to tell us what was here before?" Detective Stone asked, her brown eyes slightly bloodshot in the late morning.

John looked up at where they had indicated. They were in the central hall of the house, the one that the front doors opened into, revealing two-story ceilings, a white-stone fireplace, and a TV screen that John's father had declared "just right for the room" and John's mother had declared "monstrous." The detectives were pointing to the wall above one of the couches that sat angled to the TV, a cream expanse of drywall with a single nail driven into it a few feet up.

John blinked.

"This wasn't blank before?" Detective Stone said.

John rubbed his eyes. He tried to remember, but something in him struggled against it. *Just leave it alone*, he wanted to say. They had a murder, didn't they? Did they really need another crime? Wasn't that a little greedy?

"It was a painting, I think," John said.

"Expensive?"

"You'd have to ask my mother."

The detectives wanted him to go wake her right then; John refused, and the two sleep-deprived homicide detectives argued back and forth with him for a few minutes until John's mother emerged, bleary-eyed and still encased in her long robe.

"I'll be right down," she said when Detective Bordeaux hailed her.

Elizabeth remembered the painting exactly. A Raunert, one of his *Scenes of Stormwood,* a series made popular after a late-twentieth century discovery and brief residency in the Louvre. John remembered the painting as his mother described it to the detectives: a stormy port, a ship breaking through crashing waves, a woman, statuesque and fierce, standing alone in the rain at the rail, waiting for the ship to come in. It was done in a series of blues and golds and grays, and John had spent many an evening as a kid examining it, tracing his finger over the gilt frame as he scrutinized first the boat, and then, with even more keen interest, the unflappable, hawk-like expression on the woman.

"What's the estimated value?" Detective Stone said.

John's mother launched into some general basics about the price fluctuations of classics and the volatility of art markets, until a look from Detective Stone made her sigh and say, "Well over a million. John—my husband John—indulged me in this."

John did a double-take, looking from his mother to the detectives. A million dollars? He had been playing cars and bandits as a kid next to a painting worth *a million dollars*? His mother looked embarrassed; certainly the Eastwicks had never been overly flashy with their wealth. There was the mansion, of course, but that was inherited; their cars were always clean and respectable, but never showy. Neither of his parents cared a bit for designer brands. When John had gone to college, his parents had bought him a refurbished laptop, declaring that the electronics industry had "gone crazy" and they weren't going to "buy into the nonsense."

"You didn't know?" Detective Bordeaux said, sharp eyes on John.

"No."

"Who did? Was your brother-in-law or sister-in-law an avid art fan?" Detective Bordeaux said, turning back to John's mother.

"I—no, I don't think so. My friend Lucy, but she moved to Seattle years ago. She helped me pick this one out."

"Do you have any other paintings worth just as much?"

"Yes—two, in the master bedroom."

The detectives exchanged a look.

"What?" John's mother said. "What is it? Is it about John Sr.? Or John Jr.?"

John stepped closer to his mother and put one arm around her. She felt so cold, so frail.

"How much did Ms. Orlov know about art?" Detective Stone said. "Has she ever admired this painting?"

John's mother looked bewildered. "Tatiana? I...I'm not sure. She majored in art history, I believe."

"She must surely have noticed this painting, then."

"I can't remember. Maybe—perhaps she said something, when she was over once for an event. It would have been so many years ago, detectives. You think she did something with it?"

"We don't think anything right now," Detective Stone said evenly. "We're just trying to connect the dots. What about Ms. Jenkins or Mr. Newberry?"

"Annette never mentioned it," John's mother said. She bit the corner of a nail. "Luke? Luke knew a little, I suppose—at least, he had heard of the Stormwood series. His mother was an artist. But Luke would never—certainly he wouldn't take the painting. He's worked with us for years."

The detectives exchanged another look. "We'd like to call in some back-up," said Detective Stone. "Search the perimeter. If no one has left yet, the painting should still be on the premises."

"Oh, dear."

Just forget the painting! John wanted to shout. It would mean hours more of the police there. It would mean more questioning. It would mean no reprieve from the chaos that had so suddenly and violently entered their life.

But he also felt that they were all now trapped in some giant machine that would keep churning and chewing and destroying. He had felt that way ever since his father died. The world had torn down the middle, and nothing would ever be put back right.

CHAPTER 21

*A*nnette found Elizabeth around lunchtime. The police had requested (if it could even be called a request) that all of them stay in the house for the foreseeable future. They were searching it room by room now, and the guests had dispersed to the grounds or the basement or the banquet hall to stay out of their way. Annette had warned Luke, John, and Elizabeth to not speak to the police further without representation, advice met with varying levels of fear and disquietude.

Elizabeth was holed up in the kitchen, a mug of tea in her delicate, thin hands. She had changed into an oversized sweater and a pair of faded leggings, and in the dim kitchen light she looked smaller, younger, almost child-like. Annette took a seat next to her.

"I'm sorry for everything."

Elizabeth blinked and looked up. "Sorry?"

"John was a good man. He should have outlived us all. And the will…" Annette bit her lip. She had worked with the Eastwicks for years. She didn't want to overstep any boundaries. "It shouldn't have ended up that way. I'm not going to take the money. John paid me well—I don't need anything more."

"Nonsense, Annette. If that's what my husband wanted, that's what I want, too."

"It doesn't matter. That's what I'm doing. It's what's right." It didn't make it any easier that, by trying to be noble, Annette would be letting go of money that would just increase the fortunes of that hyena and that jackal, Edward and Vanessa Eastwick. But she couldn't help that. She had to follow her own judgment, lead where it may. "And you can meet with that estate attorney I told you about. Figure out what else you can do."

Elizabeth looked like she wanted to protest some more, but her eyes were rimmed with dark shadows, and her breathing was fluttery and light.

"I have something else to tell you," Annette said, before she could lose her nerve. "I'm leaving."

"Leaving?"

"Yes. I'm quitting my job here, and—well, if you want to know, I'm going to Hawaii, actually." Annette blushed. Even the word felt ridiculous. Frivolous. Silly. "I'm leaving the law practice."

"Oh!" Elizabeth said. "That sounds fantastic, Annette. Are you so happy?"

Annette sat frozen for a few seconds. She had expected so many reactions—she had prepared herself for anger, confusion, sadness, despair. She had not expected Elizabeth to be happy for her—to think first of Annette, and next of herself. She should have, of course. She was, after all, John Eastwick's wife.

"Yes, I'm happy," Annette said, her voice breaking. Was she? Yes, somewhere—but it was so hard to tell sometimes. Everything was such madness. "I'm leaving in three weeks. I'll sort all of my affairs here, of course, and I'll make any needed introductions—there's a great family lawyer just two towns over whom I've worked with before and highly recommend."

"Oh, don't worry about any of that," Elizabeth said.

"We'll manage. We always have. I'm not quite so helpless as I may appear." She smiled. "John did a wonderful job taking care of things. It's my turn now, I think."

Annette swallowed. And Elizabeth would have quite the time of it, too—dealing with the vultures who were equal inheritors now to her husband's estate. Annette had been so struck when she had first read the will that she had checked it again and again for fraud, scrutinized the signature, looked up the witnesses, tried to see any which way it might not be true. She wasn't a detective, but all surface markers seemed legitimate. Still, should she warn the detectives? Ask them to investigate yet a third potential crime?

She left Elizabeth to her thoughts and wandered to the backyard. The grounds sprawled out in front of her, a sea of gray and green, branches of the oak trees intertwining across the slate sky. She had always loved the Eastwick estate: it was old, and beautiful, and storybook, wild outside the walls of the white stone house, forest extending over sloping hills that led down to a breathtaking view of the water. John had had people over for yearly summer and Christmas parties over the years; more than once Annette had found herself wandering through the twisting trees out back, walking to the shore of the lake and staring out at the vast expanse of water, thinking of the extraordinary beauty of St. Clair and the subtle shadows beneath. Early on she had thought herself entranced by it, had felt that the mystery and intrigue of St. Clair only added to the town's intrigue. More lately she had begun to feel differently; she had felt herself tethered there by its charms and its magic, and worried that if she did not break free soon, she'd be entrapped by its spell forever. And staying in St. Clair forever meant staying close to those she wished to avoid.

It was only half a year ago that she had wandered down to the lake at a summer party, the last one John Eastwick had given before his death. She was flushed on rosé and kicked off her heels to sink her toes into the coarse sand of the lakeshore.

I'm going to quit, Annette had thought to herself then. *I'm going to walk up to John, tell him I'm grateful for everything, and tell him I can't do it anymore.* John knew her situation. He would understand. But the thought of his disappointment, even hurt, burst her heart. Why couldn't it have been different? Why did she have to be so weighed down by her past?

And then, from the brush—"Oh!" a voice had said, and Luke had risen from the stone he was sitting on, a sandwich in one hand and a soda in the other. He apologized, which was ridiculous, since Annette had run into him. Alcohol made her bold and deadened her own sense of embarrassment; she had encouraged him to sit back down and plopped herself onto the stone next to him. She had seen Luke around, over the years, the tall and broad-shouldered chef who spoke no more than a few words to anyone but the kitchen staff, but who made the best lemon meringue pies Annette had ever had in her life. She began to ask him about the pies, and from there they talked about Eastwick, and St. Clair, and where in the world they would move if they could.

"Hawaii," Luke had said. A dreamlike look came over his face that kindled something in Annette's heart—Hawaii! Why not? It conjured up images of the tropical, the relaxing, the beautiful. Why shouldn't she have a life like that? "I went once, when I was younger. It was the most breathtaking place I had ever seen."

"Hawaii," Annette had repeated. She thought of telling her family that she was moving to Hawaii, that she would no longer be a stone's throw away, at their beck and call. She knew how that would go over.

Somehow, impossibly, she found herself spilling all of her family history to Luke. To Luke, the quiet chef! When she had gone years, almost her whole life, hiding it. It didn't help that his blue eyes were large and understanding, that his silence invited her to talk more, without judgment, that the alcohol swirling within her made her feel ready to burst until she told him everything.

Annette had had an idyllic childhood. Her parents had been loving, sweet, encouraging. They were both lawyers, serious at work and playful at home, and took her to educational museums and libraries every weekend with earnest diligence.

It had changed when she was at college. A car crash had taken them both from her in one fell swoop: Annette found herself the sudden and unwilling inheritor of their small fortune, which she would have traded a thousand times over for her parents back.

And that was also when her Aunt Lillian moved into town.

At first, it seemed like it might be a blessing. Aunt Lillian was her mother's older sister, a serious woman who had never married and had moved across three states just to be closer to her orphaned niece. She helped handle the affairs of the funeral, soberly directing Annette on what to do and who to call and how to conduct herself. If Annette was bothered at first by those little directives about her behavior—don't cry in front of others, keep your back straighter, don't embarrass yourself by talking openly of your grief—it was drowned out by her gratitude to have Aunt Lillian in her life, especially when she felt as though she had just lost everyone.

But it only grew worse from there. After everything settled, it became clear that Aunt Lillian did not feel that the new arrangement was temporary. At an inquiry from Annette, Annette found that her aunt indeed did not even plan on moving out of her family house—it was, after all, "too big for Annette alone." Annette let her aunt know of her intention to sell the place and rent something more modest; Aunt Lillian had to be told explicitly that she was not to share the new apartment.

"Well," her aunt had said, dark-eyed and serious, "I'm not sure what you expect an old woman like me to do; I certainly can't afford these city prices on my own." Her aunt was from a semi-rural town up north, though remained vague on her affairs out there, and insisted she had nothing she needed to get back to anytime soon.

In the end, Annette had to offer to pay the first three month's rent for her aunt to agree to the separation; when those months ended, her Aunt Lillian balked at the rent and utilities ("I thought internet was included!") and let Annette know that it was at least partially her fault for suggesting the place and not being "upfront" about all of its "hidden costs." Annette paid utilities on the condo for the rest of that year and the next; when Annette went to law school and told her aunt that she could no longer afford to pay part of the bills, Annette fully expected her Aunt Lillian to move back home.

But Aunt Lillian had entrenched herself in the little town nestled outside St. Clair. She had joined a local church, dismissing the one that Annette had attended for eighteen years with her parents as "too moderate." There, Aunt Lillian had met two other women whom Annette came to call the Fates, a perhaps unoriginal moniker for three older women who spent their time knitting and gossiping about the lives of others, deriving their best and purest pleasure from pronouncing with certainty the decline of a marriage or the scandal of a neighbor. She could only imagine what the three women had said about John Eastwick, when the news came out—she had purposely avoided speaking to them for weeks now, for that and other reasons.

Aunt Lillian was so difficult precisely because, at times, she was so necessary. She was the only family that Annette had left, and she would occasionally stop by on Sundays to help Annette tidy up, even if Annette sometimes felt like these were opportunities for her aunt to disapprove of Annette's style of living. She had lunch with her niece on her birthday, and collected Annette's mail and packages when the latter was traveling so that no one else would see the apartment was temporarily unoccupied. And sometimes, like when her aunt gave one of her rare laughs, or when Annette caught a glimpse of her aunt in the sun, eyes closed, basking in the golden warmth, she could see her mother for the most fleeting second, and the ache in her heart would make her deal with a thousand Aunt Lillians for just one more such moment.

And Aunt Lillian *had* been there for her, in ways that the rest of Annette's extended family hadn't. But Annette was no longer a college student, and she no longer wished to have Aunt Lillian's advice on every part of her life.

For the bigger the subject, the larger Aunt Lillian's opinions: law, for example, was a waste of time—no one liked lawyers, anyway, and besides, all that school and they still didn't make as much as doctors? Why not be an accountant, or better yet, marry a nice gentleman and do work for the church?

And Aunt Lillian had all sorts of ideas about which "nice gentleman" her niece should end up with. Mostly older widowers and divorcés at the church, men with varying degrees of money whom Annette suspected were coveted more by Aunt Lillian and her horde of church friends than they ever would be by Annette herself. Annette found herself paraded to church every so often as the single, young, attractive creature, the light to draw the moths to the flame—and then Aunt Lillian would cast her out, tell her that the church's A.C. was broken for the next few weeks, and she had better not come back.

Once and only once did Annette try to introduce a boyfriend to her aunt. It was her second year of law school, and she was dating a very handsome third year student with a job at a prestigious local firm and a healthy admiration for Annette herself, for her work ethic and her intelligence. Annette felt very adult, being in a relationship where each partner respected the other and encouraged the other on.

"Oh," Aunt Lillian had said when she had met him, "I never imagined you'd be so short."

It wasn't much better from there. Brian was, in fact, only an inch taller than Annette, a fact that she had come to find him surprisingly insecure about, given how much he joked about it at the start of their relationship. She watched Brian's face go white, and then sat through the next three hours of similar silent jabs from Aunt Lillian, who was anything but remorseful when Brian finally ducked out and left.

"It's very hard for short men to get ahead in this world," Aunt Lillian told her. "Do you want your children to have a hard time?"

Annette and Brian broke up a few months later; he said it was the stress of starting his new job, but she had to trace the origin back to Aunt Lillian's influence. And so she had told Aunt Lillian about none of her relationships afterwards, even the one or two that grew serious enough where labels were exchanged and the future was talked about as something more concrete than fog.

And now? Now, Aunt Lillian knew nothing of what Annette was planning. She would have opinions on all of it, of course. She would try to talk Annette out of moving to Hawaii. She would lament the money Annette had wasted on her law degree (never mind that the generous Eastwick family had more than paid it off, even after just a few years). She would tell Annette that it would be more prudent to stay in town, to attend church, to pray about a new direction that no doubt would require something like volunteering part-time at the church and hungrily pursuing the latest eligible older man next. She would not understand Annette's need for sudden and whole-scale change, the need to violently rip herself from her current life if she was to have any future at all. She would snort when Annette told her that law had become dreadful to her, because she wanted a freedom that it could never provide, an independence that, by its nature, it could not give her.

("The young generation is so weak," Aunt Lillian would sneer. "Don't tell me—you're going to *follow your dreams* next, aren't you?")

Part of her felt guilty for the suddenness of her departure: Aunt Lillian had become a barnacle, yes, but she had also uprooted herself and made her whole life revolve around her niece. It wasn't healthy for either of them, and how would Aunt Lillian fill the hole?

It's not mine to worry about, Annette told herself, massaging her temples. A cold wind blew over her, and she stepped closer to the shelter of the house. She was doing what would make her happy.

Would it?

CHAPTER 22

*D*own in the banquet hall, John took his peanut butter and jelly sandwich to a far corner of the room and sat with his back to the window, as far into the shadows as he could manage. He couldn't remember the last time he had eaten; indeed, he wasn't even hungry now, but was lightheaded enough that he had finally slowed down to eat.

A murder. A stolen painting. John was too numb to fully believe it. And yet, in his heart, he felt guilty that the biggest mystery he still wanted the answer to was why his father had bribed him into Montvale.

He had received a few more texts from his friends back at school—the ones who had probably fretted and weighed whether to reach out to him, whether his radioactivity would somehow spread to them. He wondered whether they were waiting on his texts with some of their other friends, gossiping about his family and nudging each other each time the phone screen lit up, wondering what John Eastwick Jr. would have to say for himself.

John had grown up believing that his father was perfect. But he himself was not, so why should he be surprised to find his father flawed, too? John had lied before. He'd cheated on a seventh-grade geometry test by copying answer 22 from a girl named Starla. He had told a friend in high school that he couldn't be friends with him any longer, simply because a kid who seemed cooler had told John to "lose the dead weight" if he ever wanted to become popular. (Shockingly, said popularity never materialized.) John had always felt guilty about his missteps, always felt like he was too weak sometimes to live up to the high standards that his parents set. But maybe it was just genetic—part of his family. Maybe he was destined to be petty, cruel, small, self-serving.

"Mind if I join you?"

John started. Lost in his thoughts, he hadn't noticed Michael approaching him, a bowl of cereal in one hand. John nodded and kicked out one of the chairs, which Michael took.

"You look rotten," Michael said.

"I'm fine. Tired."

"Aren't we all."

They ate in silence for a few minutes. John tried to hurry himself along. He had never really minded Michael, except for the fact that he was the son of Uncle Edward and Aunt Vanessa. But he didn't like being near anyone, right now, afraid his thoughts could be read across his face. Michael seemed to notice.

"I can sit somewhere else, if you'd like."

"No. No, that's fine."

What did Michael think about the Montvale scandal? John suddenly wanted to know: he wanted to understand if his family had gloated about it, if they hated him for it, if they delighted in it. He tried to read the answer in Michael's face, afraid to speak the words: Michael had graduated from a small liberal arts school just a year ago, and worked now for a small billing agency a few towns over as he pursued his career as a movie critic. Did he think that John had always been too big for his britches? Did he relish the takedown? Had Michael, indeed, ever been jealous of John?

"Do you think I deserved it?" John blurted out.

Michael lifted one eyebrow as he took another bite of his cereal. The light from the windows fell in long strips across his face; he squinted and adjusted his seat. He didn't bother telling John that he didn't know what he was talking about. "No one deserves something like that."

"But really. Do you think.... I don't know. That I had something like that coming?"

"No, I don't." Michael hesitated. "I mean, it's not your fault. You're spoiled, but who wouldn't be, in your place? It's not your fault."

John stiffened. "Spoiled?"

"Yes. Ah, I've offended you. I didn't mean to."

"You didn't."

"I did. I can see it in your face. I don't mean you're one of those rich kids who always needs designer labels and throws a tantrum when they don't get a trip to Fiji for their birthday. I just mean, well, that you never have to deal with many problems. Everything's taken care of for you."

"Like what?"

"Bills, clothes, rent, utilities." Michael paused. "College applications."

John colored.

"I'm sorry," Michael said. "I don't mean—never mind. It's not your fault. That's the important thing."

"Is that what your parents think, too?"

Michael winced. "My parents always have colorful opinions on everything and everyone. It's never personal."

"But your dad and mine never got along anyway."

"Well, that's not exactly true. They were fine, up until The Incident."

"The party?"

Something inscrutable passed across Michael's face. "Yes. I'm sure you know the details."

"Dad just said that he and Uncle Edward had an altercation or something. He never elaborated."

Michael blinked at this. John watched as the color rose shortly to his cheeks as well. At least he wasn't the only one embarrassed.

"What?" John asked. "What happened?"

"You really never heard?"

"No."

"Does your mother know?"

"No. She asked my dad, but he wouldn't say much. I just figured that they took a few swings at each other or something."

Michael laughed harshly. "That would have been better, probably. But no, that's not what happened." He paused again. "You really want to know?"

"Sure."

Michael stared at him a few seconds longer, as if giving him the opportunity to change his mind. Then he sighed. "Your dad was not a bad guy," he said. "My dad—well, he can be rough around the edges sometimes. He's scrappy. Kind of abrasive sometimes. Not cruel, not intentionally...but anyway. My dad was drunk at the party. He was having some work trouble and, long story short, asked your dad for a job."

John nodded, feeling awkward. He knew that his father had inherited the family business, that this was at least partially responsible for the wealth disparity between Uncle Edward's family and his own, but he had never considered the possibility that Uncle Edward *wanted* to work for his father. He had always seemed to resent him, always seemed to follow him around the room with beady, serpentine eyes and a twitching mouth. Indeed, Uncle Edward had worked only briefly for the family business, before moving on to greener pastures that never seemed to materialize.

"Your dad said no, of course. They can't work together—
they'd kill each other. Well, my dad was drunk enough that he
took a swing. And missed. Toppled over in the room and
made a fool of himself. That's when my mother came into the
room."

"Aunt Vanessa?"

"The one and only. And she demanded that Uncle John
hire my dad, and—" Michael cleared his throat. "Well, ah, she
threw a glass figurine at him. I only know because I followed
her in. I was trying to get both of them to leave. It hit your
dad right in the mouth and cracked one of his teeth. My mom
started crying. My dad started talking about insurance and
lawyers and other nonsense before I could get him out. Uncle
John said he didn't need any medical attention, that he'd just
go to an emergency dentist the next morning. And a week
later, he sent my dad a significant loan to get through the next
few months."

"Well," John said, "aside from the cracked tooth, that
seemed to end pretty well."

Again, another shadow flitted across Michael's face. "The
tooth was bad, but it wasn't about that. It was—well, to be
honest, your dad could never give mine anything without
making a big deal out of it, acting like it was a charity thing. It
hurt my dad's pride. Cut him down."

"What are you talking about? I thought you just said he
gave your dad a loan?"

"Yeah, after making him sign a contract to return half of
it within three years. And if he did, the other half would be
'forgiven.' Why make a contract like that in the first place?
Why not just give him half the money, no strings attached,
and not make it so awkward for everyone?"

"I don't know. Maybe he thought he was making it easier
for Uncle Edward—official. Less embarrassing than charity."

Michael colored. "No, what's embarrassing is going into
an office with a bunch of lawyers and signing papers for a

loan from your brother, when the brother loaning you the money hasn't even bothered to show up. Like he was some loser that needed to siphon off the rest of his family in order to survive. Then again, that's probably exactly what you think of him."

"It's not."

Michael shrugged. "My parents aren't perfect. But I'd like to see anyone live in the situation that they did, for twenty years, and not be at least a little resentful."

John didn't know what to say to this. He didn't think it was fair, first of all: how did Michael expect John's father to help his family, if he thought a loan was too embarrassing? John had heard snippets over the years that had told him plainly why his father did not want to hire Uncle Edward: his uncle was lazy, bombastic, and entitled, and wanted a position well above the scope of his experience, due to the family name. Of course Uncle Edward probably saw it differently—probably felt that his older brother was stuck-up, stingy, and cruel. At the end of the day, though, did Uncle Edward really have to set himself up as the perpetual victim of his older brother's decisions? Couldn't he have made something of his life independent of what he felt he deserved from his family? Or did the knowledge that he was not granted the business sit as a thorn in his side, something Uncle Edward could never forget or move on from, something that came to define him above all else?

"Neither of our fathers are perfect," Michael said, and it seemed to John that he chose his words carefully, studying John's face as he said them. "That doesn't mean we don't love them."

Mine was perfect, John wanted to say. His heart ached. An image of his father flashed into his mind: supportive, kind, caring, patient. Michael wouldn't snatch that away from him. The world wouldn't, either.

A DEATH AT EASTWICK

"At the very least," Michael continued, "they both made mistakes."

"If you mean the college thing, I'm sure it was a misunderstanding."

"Maybe." But the look of pity that Michael gave him was unbearable.

"Even if he did it, he was only looking out for me," John said hotly. He didn't like the smug sympathy in Michael's expression—maybe, after all, that was what his cousin and aunt and uncle hated in John's family. Maybe all of this was karma.

"I'm sure he was," Michael said. "No one doubts that he loved *you*."

"And my mother. He was a great father and husband."

Michael was silent.

John's face flushed. He felt, somehow, that he had played right into Michael's hand, that Michael was directing him to all of the flaws and potential flaws of his father, bringing up rumors and hearsay to disparage John Eastwick Sr. He hated him for it, and at the same time felt disgusted with himself for being so far behind, for being blindsided by the fact that his father might have —could have—John wouldn't admit it yet—made a mistake.

"He didn't cheat on my mother, if that's what you're insinuating," John said coldly.

Michael nodded.

"Well? Is that what you're trying to say?"

Michael held up his hands. "I have no idea, John. I haven't seen him in years. It just looks weird, is all. To give her part of his estate."

"And Annette, and Luke. And you guys. He's not having affairs with all of you."

"No. But it's a good way to make it less suspicious, isn't it? Distributing the funds to a bunch of people."

"For an intelligent man, that seems like an extremely

stupid plan," John replied. He was starting to shake, all the more because of the panicky feeling running through him, the whispering doubts, *what if it's right, what if, what if...*

Michael kept watching him, his gaze intent and curious. He seemed to be waiting for John to say something else, to admit something that he knew. Perhaps, John thought, eyes widening, his cousin even thought that he had something to do with—that he had visited Tatiana and—he couldn't even force himself to finish the thought.

"Everything okay?" Michael asked. John felt as though he were lobster-red. He could barely think above the pulse in his ears.

"We wouldn't," John began, his voice scratchy and rough. "I'd never—"

The door to the banquet hall burst open. "Luke Newberry?" Detective Stone said, her sharp eyes scanning the room. Michael and John both shook their heads.

"Everything alright?" Michael asked.

"He might be in the back, near the patio," John offered.

Detective Stone said nothing. She shut the door and disappeared. Michael and John exchanged looks and then followed her out, where they ran into a group of the other guests in the kitchen.

"What is it?" John asked, moving closer to Annette, whose face was frozen in fear. "Why are they looking for Luke?"

Annette swallowed. She seemed very far off. "They found the painting," Annette croaked. "In Luke's car."

CHAPTER 23

The detectives burst upon Luke as he was scouring the backyard, sure that he had caught a glimpse of Annette out here just minutes ago. He jumped when they rushed outside and blanched when their hands flew to their hips, as if *he* were some sort of threat. Some sort of deadly threat.

"Is something wrong?" Luke asked, holding his hands half-up in mock surrender. Detective Stone and Detective Bordeaux exchanged a glance, relaxed a bit, and moved towards him.

"You should come with us," Detective Stone said.

They led him into one of the spare bedrooms and had him sit on the half-made comforter. The two detectives remained standing.

"Well," Detective Bordeaux said, crossing his arms over his chest. "Do you want to tell us anything?"

Luke looked wide-eyed between the two detectives. Had Annette spoken to them? "I don't…I'm not sure what you want me to tell you."

"Really? Nothing about the painting?"

The painting! "The stolen one?"

"That's the one."

Luke frowned. "Did you find it?"

"We did."

"Oh! Well, that's good, isn't it?"

"Indeed. And you know where we found it?"

Luke's stomach turned over. "Not in my room," he said, his voice faint.

"No, indeed," Detective Bordeaux said. Detective Stone was grim-faced and serious, watching him like a hawk. "We found it in the trunk of your car."

A wave of heat went over Luke. So that was why the detectives looked so serious. That was why they had their arms crossed in front of them, why they had acted as though Luke had been about to charge them or flee. They thought him an art thief.

"You've got it all wrong," he said, his voice deep and serious. He felt himself, in the next few moments, grow calm. It was as though he had catapulted himself right out of his terror. This was a disaster. Worse than a disaster. But he could get through it—if this was the worst of it, he could get through it.

His shoulders straightened. He listened clear-headed to the detectives as they launched a barrage of questions at him, not speaking, letting them unspool their theories and try to needle away at him. Annette used to say that this was Luke "in the zone," that it happened when he cooked more often than not. Listen, trust, act. Rely on your body when your mind was too burdened with everything else to be a reliable judge.

I'll be alright, Luke thought to himself. Because, whatever his other flaws, Luke Newberry was brave. Life had taught him that.

"I'd like to speak to a lawyer," Luke said, when Detective Bordeaux paused to draw another breath.

CHAPTER 24

*A*nnette put a stop to the questioning when the police sourly came to find her. She didn't know whether to cry or hug Luke when she saw him; she worried more whether she should ask him the inevitable question, whether he had indeed been so foolish as to take the painting off of the wall and tuck it into his trunk, thinking somehow that he could sell it and start a new life.

Annette had known of Luke's past for years. They had opened up to each other rapidly after that first party, hungry for the connection they both seemed to be lacking in their lives. Annette knew, for instance, that Luke had been raised by his mother in the suburbs on the other side of the state, and that his mother was an art aficionado, a soft-spoken woman who had been more than delighted to pass her knowledge on to her son. She knew that Luke's quiet, idyllic life had ended at the age of sixteen, when his mother had passed away and left him alone in the world, with a modest amount of money and a complete lack of direction.

Their paths in that sense were similar, though they had diverged sharply after it: Annette had gone to law school and invested her parents' money. Luke, only sixteen at the time, had made big plans for his eighteenth birthday, when he could access all of it. On that date, he made a huge withdrawal and paid for all of his friends to travel north to a resort town, where they rented kayaks and went ziplining and bought beer by playing "Hey Mister" at the various liquor stores around town.

And then? Some way or another, it went darker from there. Luke had no prospects and no remaining family. He partied with his friends. He took odd jobs that he never kept, because he still had his inheritance and because it seemed almost wasteful to be throwing away his time on a minimum-wage gig versus enjoying the fruits of the labor of his mother.

An eighteen-year-old with a little money is a rich eighteen-year-old; poverty is only determined by comparison. Luke gained a reputation among the others around his age who were not college-bound for always having the cash to buy alcohol or tobacco. Luke became popular in ways he never had before. And soon enough, that lifestyle became all-consuming.

Eventually, Luke realized that he needed another way to make money and that his current stock would not last forever. The solution that his young brain came up with was, of all things, dealing, a job that Luke, affable and popular, was surprisingly good at. At least, he was for the four years while in business—and then, at twenty-two, he was caught in a supermarket parking lot with enough pot to put down an elephant, as the cop at the time told him. He went to prison, grew angry, then grew sad, and finally grew up. When he got out, he went to work in a restaurant off the recommendation of a fellow inmate. Luke never looked back.

All of this Annette knew; she also knew that John Eastwick Sr. had been especially generous to give Luke a job. Normally, private chefs were only hired if they passed a rigid background test. He had seen something in Luke and hired him on. Not an easy decision, when Annette knew of similar stories that had ended in disaster. But now Luke was going on his tenth year at the mansion. His early mistakes had changed his personality, Annette knew: the chef that Annette and John Eastwick Sr. had met was no longer the easygoing, generous, gregarious youth: he was tight-lipped, sometimes nervous, pensive, careful. But was he a thief?

So, Annette thought, as she paced up and down the bedroom, the police would find out about the prior arrests. They were going to think that they were somehow linked to the present situation, because they always found a way to connect the dots to support their conclusions. If Annette hadn't cared about him, she would have pitied him and kept her nose clean. But now? Now what was she supposed to do?

She thought briefly of Tatiana's mocking comment, the night of the memorial service—it seemed so long ago. *Whatever it is, I hope it's been worth it. Because it won't work out.* Cutting words for a woman whom Annette had never had a problem with before. Cruel ones, too.

And what if the police found out their secret as well? They'd assume that Luke and Annette were co-conspirators, that perhaps Annette had assisted in whatever robbery Luke had or had not undertaken.

Annette swallowed.

Safest would be to disappear. To wait until all the investigations blew over, and then spirit herself out of the state, just as she had planned. But could she leave Luke to struggle in the arms of the law? She knew as well as anyone that justice was not always clear-cut, investigations not always straightforward. Especially for an ex-convict.

No, Annette thought, her heart skipping a beat. She wouldn't leave him. She couldn't abandon him right now, in large part because Annette knew that if the roles were reversed, Luke would never leave her.

CHAPTER 25

*J*ohn watched Luke and Annette leave for the police station. The police agreed that there was no longer any need for the guests of the Eastwick mansion to remain; shortly after, Uncle Edward, Aunt Vanessa, and Michael drove off as well, leaving John alone with his mother in the house.

The peace seemed stripped from their home. No longer could John walk up and down the halls, or settle into the kitchen nook near the fridge, without thinking to himself that soon all would have to be sold and divided up, that he was no longer part possessor of the place that had always been his refuge.

He supposed they'd have to start thinking about where to live next. Or would he even live with his mother, after this? He was almost a college graduate, after all: he'd need a job, scandal or not, which might mean moving to a city where his mother would not want to follow. John's stomach twisted.

He went to find his mother, who was in her bedroom again, a mug of tea clutched in her thin hands as she sat on the balcony. She reached out to squeeze his hand, smiling faintly. Somewhere in the afternoon, she had showered and changed back into her silk robe.

"This was always my favorite spot," she told him, tracing one finger along the edge of the balcony's iron railing. "Such a beautiful view."

Indeed, they could just make out the curve of the silver lake in the afternoon light.

"It's beautiful," John said. He cleared his throat. "Maybe when we move, we can look for something with a view."

His mother didn't react to this, but she did withdraw her hand from the railing, folding in on herself.

"I was thinking," John continued, "once this is all over, maybe we can look for a place. You can have my part of the estate—it should go to you anyway. We could look for a townhouse downtown, maybe, or a condo if you prefer. Would you stay in St. Clair?"

He was babbling. His mother looked at him, her expression inscrutable.

"I'm not leaving St. Clair, darling," she said finally. "Or this house."

"But the others—?"

"The house is worth quite a bit of money, yes. But I know better than anyone what your father was worth. And under my portion—especially now that Tatiana is gone—the house can still be mine. Keep yours, of course. I'll manage just fine on my own. I managed it for thirty years before I met your father."

John blinked. "But Annette said—"

"Annette said what she believed to be true. But she doesn't know your father's affairs as intimately as I do. I don't need the investment accounts, or the cash—as long as I have this house, I can cover the expenses."

John nodded. This was a version of his mother he had not expected to get; where he had expected to meet a frail bird, he instead encountered steel. It buoyed him, and at the same time broke him. He felt as though he no longer had to pretend to be the optimistic one with it all together; he wanted instead to lay his head in his hands and cry, knowing his mother would make it all right.

He didn't, though. He cleared his throat again and said, "That's good news. I still want you to have my portion, though."

John's mother pressed her lips together at this and did not answer. They sat in silence for a while longer; they had too much to talk about, and no handle to begin on any of it. *Are you angry,* John wanted to ask. *Do you wish you could speak to him one more time, ask him what he had been thinking when he made the will?* But the questions were useless: of course his mother was angry. Just as John was angry with his father. He realized it as the emotion flooded through him: yes, he believed his father had bribed the school. Maybe for some reason that seemed good at the time, maybe out of weakness. It didn't matter. John believed it and was angry with him. But that didn't change how much he loved his father. It didn't change the fact that, if he had but ten more minutes with him, he'd tell his father over and over how much he loved him, and never breathe one word of the college scandal.

But what if there was more? What if it was worse? John braced himself.

"Are you thinking about Tatiana?" he asked.

His mother turned to look at him slowly.

"It's okay," he said. "You can talk to me. I'm twenty-one. I can handle it."

"I'm sure you can, darling. But I don't have anything to tell."

A chill went through him. She was acting strange, unlike herself—John didn't want to think too hard about it. "Did you...did Dad ever talk about her?"

"No. Oh, I've run through it in my head, of course. Trying to see if there was something I missed. There might have been. When you're in a relationship, John, you have to trust the other person, which means letting each other live their lives. Were there cracks I didn't see? Pieces I didn't know about? Maybe."

"You think he had...that there was something inappropriate..." He couldn't bring himself to say it.

"Tatiana once came to me," John's mother said, turning her gaze out towards the trees, "and asked me some questions about being in love. I didn't think much of it at the time. She was giddy, just a young girl. She wanted to know how to tell if it was love or just lust. If someone truly was interested in her. I told her that you would see it by the sacrifices they made." She paused. "I wonder what she thought by the end of last night."

John felt a chill go down his spine. She was talking as though it was a fact that John's father had cheated. But it wasn't—it was all speculation. His father, the father he knew and trusted and loved, would never betray his family like that.

But he would never have bribed your way into school, either, an insidious voice whispered. John shook it off.

"Your father was an amazing man," John's mother said. "He had so many good qualities. I looked up to him. Still do." She took a deep breath and sighed. "Sometimes I wonder whether people so good have a harder time than the rest of us. It can't be an easy burden to bear."

"What do you mean?"

"Everyone is so enamored of you," his mother said. "They're blind to your faults. And you have them, of course. Everyone has them. And then what do you do? You're forced to hide them, because they've built you this pedestal that you now sit on, and you can't let everyone down. But when the lies come out, when the pedestal falls..." She sighed. "I'm so sorry. I'm just going on and on."

John analyzed his mother in the fading afternoon light.

The doors to the master bedroom were wide open, so that heat and warmth spilled over them from behind and an occasional frosty gust of wind blew towards them from the front. His mother looked tired, yes, but serious, thoughtful. And that layer of steel she had shown him earlier...what, indeed, was his mother capable of?

CHAPTER 26

𝒯he light in the windowless interrogation room was low; Annette blinked to adjust her eyes more rapidly, and tried not to breathe too deeply of the stale air that smelled of carpet cleaner and hand sanitizer. They had given her the rickety chair, which seemed a little clichéd, and had kept her waiting for a good twenty minutes.

Finally the door opened, and Detective Stone stepped in. Annette's gaze wandered over to the large mirror on one side. Again, she thought, clichéd. Detective Stone slid into the seat opposite her.

"So you're planning to represent him, then?" Detective Stone said. "I didn't think you were that type of lawyer."

"I don't expect the charges to hold," Annette said, with a confidence she didn't feel. Never mind the fact that the attorney thing was a bluff—no judge would let Annette represent Luke, under the circumstances. "Of course, if things go further, he can seek other counsel. I'm here as a friend."

Detective Stone nodded. Annette wondered how old she was: younger than Annette, certainly, possibly early thirties. Too young to be looking that tired. Did she have a family? Good friends? How had she ended up in St. Clair, of all

113

places? Annette's eyes slid to the detective's hands, but as if sensing the direction of her thoughts, Detective Stone slid her hands back to her lap and began talking.

"Let's talk as friends, then," Detective Stone said. "Mr. Newberry is saying he always leaves his car unlocked."

"Why wouldn't he? He works at the Eastwick place. They have a rock-solid security system."

"And yet, no cameras in the garage. Would Luke have known that?"

"I'm his lawyer right now, detective. If I knew anything incriminating about him, I wouldn't tell you."

"Let's say yes. Anyone else in that house know about the lack of cameras?"

"I don't see why not."

"But you don't know."

"I thought," Annette said, "that we were talking as friends. But even if the car was locked—and I don't think it was— you've seen where all the keys hang, haven't you? It would be just as easy for someone to pick one at random and place the painting in the trunk of another car. Especially if the police were prowling around."

"And what if that person drove off with it?"

"Not likely, given that you had asked us all to stay put."

Detective Stone smiled and leaned forward. "Maybe," she said. "We've considered that, too. I'm guessing, since you're friends with Mr. Newberry, you know all about his past arrests."

"Arrest, singular. He did some time for it."

"Two arrests. The first time he was released, no charges. The second time, jail."

Annette blushed. She hadn't known that—why hadn't Luke told her that? But she wouldn't let herself be bested, not now, not over that. "Fine. Yes, I knew he was in jail. That was years ago. He was a kid."

"Seems he had quite the reputation in jail. Swiped food, supplies, letters from other inmates."

Luke had told her about that, at least. He would bake pies as a way to pass the time; the other inmates loved them, but no one usually wanted to fork up the money or ingredients necessary to have one. It became something of a game, a prank: Luke would take what he needed, trying to evenly distribute the losses among the inmates, so that one would lose a few quarters here, another a bar of chocolate there, until he had enough to buy or make what he needed. If anyone raised a fuss, Luke paid them back, or someone else paid them off. It was all harmless, in good fun. Wasn't it?

"He never stole letters," Annette said, stomach twisting as she waited for Detective Stone to contradict her.

The detective waited a few beats, then smiled. "No, not letters. Cake-making, was it? Has he ever cooked for you, Ms. Jenkins?"

"Of course. I'm a frequent guest of the Eastwick house."

"That's not what I mean."

Annette held Detective Stone's gaze. Her heart thumped in her chest; now was the moment when she had to make a decision.

"Yes," Annette said. "We dated, for a time."

"Ah. When did that start?"

"A year ago. We're not seeing each other anymore."

"Hmm." Detective Stone leaned forward in her chair. "Can I ask why not?"

Why not? Annette had run over that question in her own head many times. Perhaps because her Aunt Lillian was too crazy to foist on anyone that Annette cared about, and Luke had been dropping hints that he'd like to meet her family. Perhaps because he was a formerly incarcerated chef and she was a lawyer, and part of her was indeed as stuck-up as Luke feared, when he had initially demurred when she had asked him to lunch. "Girls like you aren't serious about boys like me," he had said, and she had fallen in love with him just a little that day, and a lot more in the weeks and months to come.

But mostly they were not together because Annette had decided to break free, and because to do so she knew that she couldn't try to drag anyone with her. It might be the greatest mistake of her life to move to Hawaii, and if it was, she didn't want anyone else's life torpedoed along with hers. She needed to get away from St. Clair, for her own sanity.

She had told Luke that, in not so many words. "I'm moving," she said. And before he could process the first words, "So we'll have to break up."

His crestfallen face had haunted her dreams. And more so, the way he had stiffened, the way a wall had slammed over his face almost immediately, as if he had expected this from the very start. Maybe he had. "Oh," Luke had said, voice cold. "I'm sorry to hear that."

That had been three weeks ago. A dozen times Annette had picked up the phone since then, wondering if she could make it right. A dozen times she had put it back down, resolved not to prolong Luke's agony anymore, in case she kept changing her mind.

"Sorry," Annette said, rousing herself. "What was the question?"

"When did you two break up?"

"A few weeks ago. It wasn't—well, we didn't break up, not in a bad way. It's just, I'm moving. To Hawaii."

"Ah. Congratulations." Detective Stone assessed her as Annette shrugged. "And how did Mr. Newberry take that?"

"Well. Very well. He wasn't—we're older, Detective. Not hotheaded, anymore."

"Luke is thirty-four, isn't he?"

A good seven years younger than Annette herself. "Old enough."

Detective Stone grinned at that. She shuffled some papers

and sighed. "Well, Ms. Jenkins. I think we're almost done here."

"Good. When will Luke be released?"

"Soon. Very soon. My partner is just chatting with him."

"Good." Annette made a move to rise, but Detective Stone signaled to her to wait. Frowning, Annette slid back down.

"Before you go," Detective Stone said, "I'd just like you to tell me what it is you're holding back."

Annette blushed. "Nothing."

"Nothing?"

"I've already told you we were dating. No one knows that." Except Tatiana, perhaps. Somehow…

"Right. And there's nothing else? Nothing else at all that you think I should know?"

It's a trick, Annette reminded herself. A trick to try and pull something else out of her, make her think that they had more than they did. They couldn't possibly know… She hadn't said a word to anyone, had barely even let herself think the thought… Annette rose.

"I think we're done," she said.

Detective Stone watched her in silence as she strode out.

CHAPTER 27

etective Bordeaux sat next to Luke, moving through some of the case files with him. He pointed out the picture of the garage, lingered over the photo of Luke's sedan trunk open with the painting inside, let Luke catch one glimpse of a case report with words like *prime suspect* and *suspected deception* on it before Detective Bordeaux snatched it away.

"I'm sure you know it looks bad," Detective Bordeaux said. Luke's expression remained stiff, unyielding. "Your friend is in the other room. Want me to go get her?"

"Annette?"

"Yes." Luke's face lit up; Detective Bordeaux almost did feel sorry for the guy. But then Luke slumped back in his chair, crossing his arms.

"It doesn't matter," Luke said. "I'm not saying anything."

"We'll get her nonetheless," Detective Bordeaux said. He leaned in a little closer. "Want to know one of my theories in the meantime?"

Luke shrugged.

Detective Bordeaux tapped the picture of Luke's trunk.

"It's a little too convenient, don't you think? This ending up in your car?"

No response.

"Have you been thinking to yourself how the painting ended up there? Who might think that your trunk would be a good hiding spot?"

Luke dropped his gaze but still said nothing.

"Maybe someone who thought they'd have access to it later," Detective Bordeaux said carefully. He watched Luke, but the big chef still did not respond. "Maybe someone who was close to you. Who trusted you."

His words hit home. He could see it in the redness that crept up the chef's face and neck. Poor guy, Detective Bordeaux said. Maybe he didn't have anything to do with it after all.

"Do you know anyone who might fit that description?" Detective Bordeaux pressed.

Luke raised his eyes, finally. He held Detective Bordeaux's gaze for a few beats. In them the detective saw something wild, fierce, willful. "No," Luke said. "No one at all."

Detective Bordeaux rolled his tongue over the back of his teeth. That wouldn't do. "Listen," he said, leaning forward. "You're not a first offender. Someone who was—the law would be more lenient with them. If your hands are clean, you shouldn't try to protect—"

"If you try to say one more time that she had anything to do with it," Luke said, his voice stronger and lower than anything Detective Bordeaux had yet heard from him, "I'll lie until you can't figure out which way is up."

"You mean take the fall."

Luke said nothing, only glared at him.

"Even if she betrayed you?" Detective Bordeaux said. "Because I'm sorry, Luke, but you haven't heard what's going on in that other room. You don't know what she's saying to us. In fact, confidentially, I'd say you'd probably do well getting yourself another lawyer." He'd have to, anyway. No way the station would allow one suspect to be the lawyer for another. Not that they had told either Luke Newberry or Annette Jenkins that, yet.

"Annette would never betray me," Luke said.

"Are you sure about that?"

A shadow passed over Luke's face. His whole expression seemed to tremble. "I'm done," he said.

CHAPTER 28

*T*he next night passed slowly for John. The police had called to update him and his mother, or so they said, noting that the preliminary results were back and that Tatiana had been poisoned. Whether it was possible for preliminary autopsy reports to be back after two days John didn't know: he didn't trust the police, expected that they were really just gauging his reaction, and hung up the phone when they started probing about what medications his mother was on.

"We'll have to get a lawyer," John said, as matter-of-factly as he could, when he sat down to finish dinner with his mother. She looked pale and ruffled, and didn't respond. John felt another chill go through him.

"What did they say?" she asked. "Have they arrested someone?"

"No. They didn't tell me anything about Luke or the painting."

"He didn't steal it. That's nonsense."

"Right. But they said Tatiana—they said she was poisoned." He found himself, against his will, watching his mother's reaction. She twirled a forkful of pasta around on her plate, delicate wrist swishing back and forth.

"Poisoned," his mother repeated.

John swallowed. He felt sure that if the detectives were to spirit his mother away for questioning, she would give them that same dazed look, repeat their questions in that same dreamy tone, which did nothing to allay any suspicions and did everything to make her seem like a woman for whom reality had become warped and tragic. What might such a woman be capable of?

"I'm calling a lawyer in the morning," John said firmly. "We're not going to talk to the police anymore unless one is present."

"That's nice," his mother said.

The next morning, John set off at the crack of dawn.

He left a voicemail for a local criminal attorney on his way, too anxious to wait until nine a.m. for someone to be in. He thought of his mother, wondered what she'd think of his brief note about getting groceries, wondered if she was in any state to care. He felt his stomach flip again: he had lost one parent already; could he lose two?

It took him all of twenty minutes to arrive at his father's office. John Eastwick Sr. had bought one of the beige-brick historic buildings downtown, leasing the offices out to obstetricians and accountants and even a yoga studio (though the last had since folded and been replaced by a "Baby Ballet" studio a year ago). His offices were at the top of the building, with a breathtaking view of the main street and, on the horizon, a thin sliver of the lake. John had watched many a parade with his parents from the offices, had gone with his father to work when he was a kid and sat at an empty desk, typing up fake reports and binding them with the spiral plastic coils that his father's old secretary, Mrs. Ramirez, had offered him with faux solemnity, promising him that a "company-wide meeting" would assess his findings later.

Now John climbed the steps to his father's office with a heavy heart. John Eastwick Sr. had always been a big believer in keeping his team small and lean: besides his secretary, he had only two other employees in the office, both junior associates that he had planned to make equal partners one day. He had trained them since they had graduated college ten years ago; one, Poppy, was a dark-haired girl with neatly tailored suits and a sleeve tattoo who hailed from the west coast. The other, Tyrone, was an Ivy League graduate with family nearby who had taken the job to be close to his sister after a difficult accident. John wasn't even sure if he would find them at work: part of him expected the office to have vanished the moment his father died, sucked up in the vortex of destruction the loss of John Eastwick Sr. had caused.

The office was unlocked. John slipped inside and found Poppy and Tyrone both seated at the white table in the center of the office, heads bent low together. They jerked up as the door opened; John swore that he saw something like fear in Poppy's eyes.

"My goodness!" she said, pale hand pushing back a wave of dark hair. "You frightened us! I thought you were a ghost."

"How are you doing?" Tyrone said, recovering first. He held out a chair for John. "Can we help you find something?"

"Sort of," John said. He took a breath. "I want you to tell me about Tatiana."

CHAPTER 29

*P*oppy and Tyrone exchanged a glance.

"Tatiana?" Poppy said. "What about her?"

First off, why she was included in my father's will, and you two weren't, John thought, but he bit his lip. He couldn't bear to even insinuate anything bad about his father in front of these two; what if he saw confirmation, or worse, pity, in their eyes?

He wasn't ready. Not yet.

"I'm so sorry to hear about what happened," Tyrone said into the silence. His eyes, wide set and thick with lashes, remained fastened on John's. He had always been a serious, thoughtful person: he "engendered instant trust," as John's father liked to say. "And the memorial service—we wish we had been back in time. We only just got back from our meeting with the London client, and we're supposed to meet with the company lawyer today to discuss...but never mind that." He hesitated. How is your mother?"

"She's fine. I just—I want to find out what happened. Why Tatiana...she was murdered, you know."

Poppy and Tyrone again exchanged a glance.

"We did hear about that. Can we help?" Poppy finally said. "Do you need to look in your father's desk, or...?"

"No. It's okay, thanks. I just want to know what she was like." He took a breath and forced himself to say it. "How she was at work, and—and how she got along with my father."

If they suspected an affair, they didn't show it: both of their faces remained concerned but blank. "She was a nice girl," Poppy said. "Smart. Worked hard. Really reliable, which your dad always likes in an employee. She used to give him three days' notice about being sick—she always said she could feel it 'coming on.'"

Tyrone grinned at that, but seemed to sober when he remembered the circumstances. "She kept to herself a little bit," he said. "Poppy and I tried to invite her out for drinks, but she was busy, usually. But she was funny, the couple of times she did come. Good sense of humor—cracked jokes all the time."

"Did she get along with my dad?"

"Of course. Your dad was a great boss. Always wanted to make sure that we were happy, regular raises, good benefits."

"Kind, motivational, not a micromanager," Poppy listed off. John struggled within himself. As much as he was hungry to hear more praise of his father, to hear that his two employees didn't think ill of him after the college scandal, he had more to find out. More he needed to know.

"What about, like, interpersonally? Did she feel the same way as you two?"

Poppy and Tyrone again exchanged a glance. John colored. He knew it wouldn't be long before the two of them guessed the direction of his line of questioning. "She liked him," Poppy said. "I think they had maybe a couple of disagreements over the years she worked here. I never knew really what about."

"I think one of them had to do with a document that was printed in color by Tatiana. John—your father—liked everything black and white."

"Oh, yes," Poppy said. "Goodness! I think she sulked for

three days about that. That was early on. But she never color-coded anything again."

Was that why she was sulking? Or had they had some sort of quarrel—some sort of *personal* fight?

"And she always looked up to your father," Poppy said. "She always spoke highly of him, and you and your mother, too. I think she wanted her own family to be like that one day. Didn't she say something like that to us, Tyrone?"

"Hmm? When?"

"Oh, I don't know—a few weeks ago. She said that she wanted a close-knit family, like John's."

Tyrone shrugged. "Sounds vaguely familiar."

"Right," Poppy said, rolling her eyes. "Well, she did. And I think it was on her mind because—well, I don't have anything to back this up, but I think she was engaged."

"Engaged!" Tyrone said.

"Yes. She told me a few months ago she was seeing some-one, but she was so sparse on the details. She said that she couldn't go public yet, because it wasn't the right time—that they had to wait a little longer. She's young enough that that sort of nonsense would have seemed romantic to her."

John didn't know what to say. Would his father even be capable of something like that? And would Tyrone and Poppy recognize it if he were?

"What made you think she was engaged?" John croaked.

"Oh, just in the way she talked about it," Poppy said. "That she couldn't announce it yet, until something else happened. You don't really announce relationships—at least, I think you don't—but you do announce engagements."

"What was the something that needed to happen?"

Poppy frowned. "She was vague. It was—I'm not sure. Something to do with family. Maybe her fiancé had to talk to his family first? I don't know."

Family. Or, the man had to divorce his wife.

Tyrone was watching John closely. "What are you worried about?" he asked. "Something's on your mind."

"It must be a lot," Poppy said, reaching out to squeeze John's forearm. "Your father's sudden death, then Tatiana's… it's been hard for us, and we're even a few degrees removed. You know your father wanted you to take over the fund when he passed away?"

John nodded. "But it's not in the will, so it likely is going to be liquidated. Before being split seven ways." Poppy and Tyrone exchanged a confused glance, and John, blushing deeper, told them briefly of the surprise scene of the other night: a will so wholly unlike anything John or his mother had expected. Poppy and Tyrone were especially surprised to hear that Tatiana was named as the inheritor of a share.

"It's not that I'm jealous," Poppy said. "But really—well, maybe I am jealous. But socially, at least, we were a lot closer to your father. Tatiana was all business."

"That can't be right," Tyrone said, frowning. "You're sure there's no mistake?"

"Not that I know of."

Tyrone rose and walked into the street-facing private office a few feet away. He returned a few moments later, shaking his head. "I know your dad kept some personal documents in there," he said. "I'll check around for a copy of the will. I feel like he mentioned it before."

"That's right," Poppy said. "I remember him saying something a few months ago. Something about an updated will. Maybe the note about you running the business is in there, too."

John shrugged. He couldn't worry about running his father's business, not now: not when he had been kicked out of college. His dad had meant years in the future—when presumably John would have had some form of master's degree and a few years of experience under his belt, preferably at a prestigious consulting company or private equity group out on the East Coast. The thought of him trying to work with Tyrone and Poppy, let alone manage them, was completely laughable. And besides, how was he supposed to manage his father's investment business—dependent as it was on relationships—when his father's reputation had been so completely torpedoed?

"We'll find it," Tyrone said. "I'm sure it says what his plans were for the business."

"That's kind of you. But the one that they read us was updated—at least according to my mom. If I were you, I'd start looking for other jobs."

"We'll wait for the will," Poppy said, a little nervously. "Your father was always careful—he'll have planned for this."

"Sometimes not careful enough," John said, and then wished he hadn't. He blushed; by the way Tyrone and Poppy were looking at him, it was obvious that they knew what he meant.

"We all make mistakes," Poppy said.

"Even big ones," Tyrone said. "I'm sure if he was around, he'd have wanted to atone for it."

"Sure," John said.

"Wait," Poppy said. "You guys don't think—I mean, with Tatiana, you're not suggesting—?" She blushed. "Sorry, John. I feel bad for even thinking it, but you're not thinking—you don't believe he was having a romantic relationship with her, do you?"

"I don't know."

Tyrone gave Poppy a pointed look before turning back to John. "Look, John, that's none of our business at all anyway— but I don't think that's the case. Really. Your dad has passed; there's no reason to think about that stuff at all."

"That'd be nice, but there *is* a murder investigation," John said. Poppy and Tyrone exchanged another glance. Were they holding something back? He couldn't tell; his instincts were off. He didn't know if his father's two employees were trying to be kind now that his father had died or if they really did believe an affair was impossible. John wasn't naïve; he knew that even if his father had never treated Tatiana preferentially, that didn't mean that one night, one mistake, couldn't have happened. Couldn't have led to other consequences.

"And how is it going?" Poppy asked, hesitating. "The murder investigation, I mean."

"It's going." He told them briefly of that night, and then the discovery of the missing painting in the morning. To his surprise, Poppy's eyes widened when he spoke of the painting.

"I remember that," she said. "You know who pointed it out to me? Mentioned it was valuable?"

John swallowed, hoping she wouldn't say Luke. "Who?"

"Tatiana! Said it was her favorite painting. 'Stormwood,' wasn't it? She studied art history in school, I think. But the police caught the thief?"

"Well, they found the painting. But they don't know who stole it yet." He wouldn't even mention where it had been found—he didn't want to believe the kind chef was capable of that kind of cruelty, the night after receiving a large portion of his father's estate.

"Weird," Poppy said. "But they must think it's related— the murder and the theft, right? Do you think Tatiana was trying to take it? That someone surprised her, and...?"

A loud knock on the door made all three of them jump. Tyrone motioned for them to stay still and walked over to the peephole on the front of the office door. He turned back quickly. *Police*, he mouthed, and motioned for John to go towards the back exit. John rose, heart beating. He didn't know why, exactly, but he felt sure the police would not be thrilled to find him chatting with his father's former coworkers —with Tatiana's former coworkers. He squeezed Poppy's hand back when she reached out to grab his and returned her warm smile with a meek one of his one. Then, with a wave to Tyrone, he moved to the back staircase, the door shutting behind him just as he heard Tyrone's booming, "Officers! How can I help you?"

John felt sick as he moved downstairs. He had gotten no firm answers, only worrisome implications. Had Tatiana indeed thought herself engaged, or nearly so, to his father? Had she stolen the painting that night, and been discovered? And if so, who was most likely to have found her spiriting away the painting? Who was most likely to have confronted her, and taken revenge?

CHAPTER 30

"*W*hat if Tatiana wasn't the target?" Detective Stone said, shuffling through papers at her desk. She and Detective Bordeaux were sorting through notes, photographs, and interview transcripts. Well, she was, as Bordeaux doodled on the giant whiteboard he had bought as soon as he had been promoted to detective, because apparently he had watched too much television and thought solving a murder required at least a few dozen lines of marker script.

"Hmm?" Bordeaux said, dashing off another column, this one labeled 'Suspects.'

"What if Tatiana wasn't the target of the poisoning? What if it was someone else? Her drink was poisoned, wasn't it? And a lot of them were drinking wine. If her glass got switched…"

"But that doesn't make any sense," Bordeaux said, frowning. "She was having an affair—"

"Allegedly."

"What are you, a lawyer? *Allegedly*, she was having an affair with John Eastwick Sr. And then she gets an equal share of his estate as his wife and kid does. If that's not motive enough for murder, I don't know what is."

135

"Assuming the wife or the kid did it."

"You don't think they did?"

Detective Stone bit her pen. She could see the noose slipping around Mrs. Eastwick, and the woman certainly hadn't done herself any favors in the interview. She had by turns been defensive, spacey, and resigned.

"I know they're sympathetic," Bordeaux said kindly. "That doesn't mean they're clean. Sometimes good people do awful things."

Detective Stone knew it, but it didn't make it any easier to bear that truth.

CHAPTER 31

*V*anessa applied coconut moisturizer to her face as
Edward slammed drawers in the bedroom. He was
making a fuss just like a little child, waiting for her to ask him
what was wrong.

She was tired of it.

Always she had to be mothering him. Always she had to
be soothing him, after every failure or slight. Always she had
to be encouraging him, telling him that yes he deserved it, yes
he ought to get what was his, yes he ought to ask for that
promotion, secure that pay raise, tell that subordinate where
to put his suggestions. Why couldn't men handle their business? What in the world would they do without women?

She had just finished with her moisturizer and was tying
her hair up when Edward pushed open the door to the master
bathroom and planted his feet in front of her with his arms
crossed.

"Yes?" Vanessa murmured, running her fingers through
her hair with the elastic clasped between pursed lips.

"These damn delays! It's unconstitutional."

"I'm sure it's perfectly legal."

Edward swore. "Don't give me that, Vanessa. You're panicking just as much as I am."

"Panicking?" Vanessa said, swinging around to him. "Surely you're not talking about the money. Because we have no reason to *panic*. Not that I know."

She watched him. Edward scowled. She tried to figure out if he was just being dramatic, or if there was indeed something that he hadn't yet told her. For heaven's sake, she thought. Not another debt. She had access to all the credit cards. He had agreed not to sign up for anything else independently. What was it?

"Don't look at me like that," Edward snapped. "You're always judging me. The only reason I got those credit cards in the first place was to pay for house repairs! The ones that *you* kept nagging me to do."

"I'd prefer not to live with bricks falling down around me and pipes leaking water through the ceilings," Vanessa said coolly. She could feel the grooves clicking into the familiar lines of their arguments: never enough money, always someone else's fault. Always *her* fault, in Edward's eyes. Once he had had the nerve to tell her that she should have kept her career after she had had Michael, that if she hadn't wanted to be one of those "pilates and ponytail" moms, then maybe their family would be in a better situation. She had thrown a houseplant at him.

"I always do whatever you tell me to. But it's never on your timeline, is it? If I don't do it the second you mention it, you'll call a plumber and expect me to pay the bill."

She knew her next line: he never did anything ever until Vanessa threatened to call someone, and sometimes not even then. But she didn't want to get into this argument. It wasn't the time. "Edward," she said, "do we need money immediately? You have to let me know."

Edward colored. "Well, I was *expecting* a little something by now," Edward muttered. "There's that tuckpointing company —the one you insisted had to come out last year."

"I thought we had paid them."

"That's because you always thought the job would only cost a few thousand dollars," Edward said bitterly. "Twelve thousand, Vanessa. They wanted twelve thousand."

"Didn't you get more than one quote? Seriously, Edward—"

"There you go again! Think I have all the money in the world to redesign the place, don't you! No skin off your nose!"

"Tuckpointing the bricks *out of safety concerns* is hardly redesigning." Vanessa's lips tightened, and she spoke quickly before Edward could let out his next breath. "How much? Are they going to put a lien on the house?"

"If they haven't already," Edward huffed. "Six thousand."

"Six thousand!"

"That's if they waive the interest they're threatening us with," Edward said. "And then of course there's the mortgage, and the cable you wanted, and the heat bill is just going up now that it's winter…I *assumed* it would be taken care of by now."

"It's not my fault the night went sideways," Vanessa snapped. "And we have the inheritance coming, don't we? We just have to make it work until then."

"You don't understand, do you?" Edward said, with a maniacal smile that made Vanessa think he was deriving some sadistic pleasure from this. "It could be months before we see any of that money. Months! And with the murder, who knows how long it will take. And if John and Elizabeth try to sue us—"

"Sue us!"

"Why not? They're greedy little devils, aren't they? Will do anything to keep their claws in John's money."

Vanessa squeezed her ponytail tighter and let her hands drop. She felt as though the air had been knocked out of her.

Some things had gone wrong, yes, but on the whole she had started to think their luck was turning around. Of course she should have known better. Of course John Sr. would still have some way to screw them over, even beyond the grave. Maybe he had just given them the gift to watch them squirm and fight to secure it, knowing full well the will would never hold up in court. Would it? They needed a lawyer, but they couldn't afford one, not now. They were going to Aspen next month, for heaven's sake! What if the money hadn't come in by then?

"Let's just keep calm," she said finally. "Lay low. The money will come."

"Long-term," Edward said. "What about short-term?"

Vanessa thought. "Take a mortgage out against the house," she said. "A second mortgage. It will give us enough cash to tide us over."

"Assuming the money from the will comes through."

"It's a legal document, Edward. Of course it will."

Edward sneered at this, but in the end left her alone. She heard him hail Michael, his voice changing from whining and frustrated to hearty and buoyant. If only he knew how much Michael despised him, Vanessa thought, gathering her purse. Their son was old enough now to understand how poorly Edward had mismanaged their lives. Vanessa had talked with him about it, a few times—carefully, hints here and there, never outright throwing Edward under the bus. Michael wouldn't respect her if she did. But he knew that they could have been much better off, *would* have been much better off, if Edward had made some different choices in life.

Vanessa hated John Sr. for a thousand little reasons that made it hard to articulate, in the cumulative, why she felt so passionately against him. Part of it was the contrast to her own husband, surely, and part of it the way that it had all gone down—the brief flirtation, the introduction to Elizabeth, the dawning realization over the years that Vanessa had ended up with the wrong Eastwick, had been robbed of her proper life. But it wasn't just her own jealousy that made her hate John, no matter how much that would have flattered him. She hated him because he made it clear, year after year, just how superior he felt himself and his family to be. He offered to help out with finances only when in the company of other people—at parties, Christmas dinners, at a wedding reception. His charity always came with a jab; he would be generous if he could put you in your place at the same time. Of course Edward and Vanessa never accepted that.

Worst of all was how he treated Michael. Vanessa could never forgive him for it. Just last year, she had gotten a near-hysterical phone call from Michael, her even-tempered and kind son, asking her to pick him up from John Sr.'s office. She had rushed over to find Michael nearly in tears, out in the alley behind the brick downtown office, John red-faced beside him. "If I ever catch you here again," John was saying, but then Vanessa began shouting at him, and John began shouting at her, and it only ended when John's office minions had come down and escorted their boss back upstairs. Tatiana had lingered near Michael, fluttering, trying to hand him a hand-kerchief, apologizing, but Vanessa had told her coldly that they didn't need her help and led Michael off.

And what was the reason for such callous treatment of his own family? Michael had gone over there simply to talk about a summer internship. Vanessa had been flabbergasted. Michael told her the story as she drove him home, though at first he was reluctant. He was out of college already, but he plainly saw the career advantages of working at a place like Eastwick Ventures. He had gotten to the office early; Tatiana had allowed him to wait nearby, rather than kicking him out to the street. And what had John Sr. done when he had arrived? Accused her son of trying to steal company property! Of spying! Now that Vanessa had heard some choice rumors about Tatiana, she had a better idea of what might have been going on: John had seen the young, handsome Michael speaking to his mistress and gone wild with jealousy. Because John Eastwick Sr. couldn't share a damn thing.

Vanessa slung her purse over her shoulder and headed downstairs. Sometimes, in moments like this, when she reviewed all of life's little injustices, considered all of the hardships that she daily had to overcome, Vanessa felt rage bubble up within her, caustic and boiling. She would do anything, anything at all, to protect her family. She would kill for her family, if she had to—she wasn't ashamed to realize it. Edward was different, though. Edward was a coward. A sneaking coward who hid bills and responsibilities until they blew up in his face.

No matter, Vanessa thought. She would fix things, as she always had. She slid into her car and started the engine. First, she had one of her regular appointments at the massage parlor.

CHAPTER 32

The idea came to Elizabeth as she was sorting her husband's clothes into neat piles: discard, donate, and give to John Jr. It was chilly in the large house, and it would take at least a few hours for the radiators to shudder awake and release their steam-driven heat. She stoked a fire instead and stood nearby, in one of her bathrobes, with her hands outstretched. Its flames were mesmerizing, and she thought: *well, it's as practical as anything*.

She couldn't tell if this was a rational thought. It seemed she was having fewer and fewer of those these days. But Elizabeth went upstairs, picked up all of the clothes in her "discard" pile, and walked back down to the fire.

She began to throw them in, one by one.

The flames sizzled in a most satisfying way, and Elizabeth found that she very much enjoyed watching the clothes burn and shrivel up, disappearing into the ravenous fire. Better than a landfill, wasn't it? And it was so tidy, too. John Sr. had been cremated: watching the clothes disintegrate into nothingness, Elizabeth could almost believe they weren't being destroyed at all, but just beamed up to wherever John was now, uncomfortable and naked while he waited for them.

"Mom?" a voice from the kitchen said. "What are you doing?"

She looked up. John Jr. walked into the living room, a peanut butter sandwich suspended in one hand. Groceries! She had to remember to buy groceries. Luke couldn't, obviously, what with being arrested and all. She must remember to call Luke. Was he out yet? Should she try the police precinct?

John Jr. walked over and snatched the clothes from her hands. She smiled at him. "Darling, those are in the 'discard' pile."

"Dad's clothes?"

"I'm donating some, giving you some, and getting rid of the rest." She motioned to the fire.

The level ten alarm in John Jr.'s eyes seemed to shift down to something like a five. Poor John! He had enough to be worried about. He didn't really have to worry about her. She wanted to tell him so, but she felt tired suddenly and collapsed onto the couch.

"Let's just hold off on this for now," her son said, lowering himself into the seat next to her. "Maybe we can donate some of the clothes first, then worry about discarding the rest."

Elizabeth nodded. "I have a system, darling. I'll take care of it." She didn't want to become one of those widows who let her children take over for her husband, who was so absorbed in her grief that she wouldn't allow herself to take on any responsibilities at all. It was self-indulgent, unacceptable.

And yet she was so tired...

"I spoke to Poppy and Tyrone today," John Jr. said. "I stopped by the office."

"Oh! Lovely. And how are they?"

"Fine." He paused. "I asked them about Tatiana."

Elizabeth felt something deep within her stir, something that was still hibernating. She pushed it down. "What about?"

He held her gaze for a few seconds. He wanted something from her, she could tell. But Elizabeth had nothing to give him. Nothing she could or would say to her child about the awfulness of the past few days. So she just blinked at him, wide-eyed, waiting.

John drew himself up.

"I wanted to know what it was like between her and dad," John said.

"Between Tatiana and your father?"

"Yes."

"And? What did Poppy and Tyrone say?" The flames still crackled behind John; Elizabeth had the urge to get up and saunter over to them, until its dry heat pressed against her legs, sizzled over her bare knees.

"They didn't know much. They thought—they were surprised by the will." Another pause. "Were you?"

Oh, John, she wanted to say to him. She wanted to draw him near to her, to make him rest his head on her shoulder. She wanted to comfort him the way she could when he was just a little baby, when she was his entire world and could make everything better simply by promising that it would be so. But now? Now, she had no such power. Now, she had to fervently hope that whatever darkness lurked in the past would stay well in the past, and not disturb their tortured present any further.

"Yes," Elizabeth said, massaging her throat. "I was surprised."

"Were Dad and Tatiana...close?"

"Oh, John—"

"You can tell me. I'm not afraid to hear."

But he was! Oh, poor child, he was. He was nearly trembling on the sofa. Elizabeth had to force herself not to reach out to him; he wouldn't like that. He would want her to believe him, that he was fine.

"They didn't seem especially close to me," Elizabeth said finally. "Oh, Tatiana came over for parties sometimes, and some Christmas events. Just like Poppy and Tyrone did. I

145

suppose I always had the impression that she was a bit cold—
of course, it doesn't mean anything. It's hard to read people's
hearts when they're hellbent on deceiving yours."

She smiled weakly at John, but he didn't return it. His eyes
remained fixed upon hers.

"So you think...?" he said cautiously.

"Maybe there was something," Elizabeth said. Her voice
was barely a whisper. How often had she tortured herself with
this possibility over the last few days? "Possibly, there could
have been. Your father has never—that is, I've always known
him to be a loyal man. But if there was anything, it doesn't
change how much he loved us."

She didn't say the rest: didn't tell John that over the last
few days, Elizabeth had thought long and hard about the
possibility of her husband being a cheater—an *adulterer*, more
specifically. She thought of how popular he was with the
opposite sex before they had gotten married, how on their
honeymoon the waitress had slipped John her number and
they had had a good laugh about it that night. She thought of
one day, many years back, when John Jr. was just a child,
when she had received a phone call from a woman with a soft
voice on the other end of the line. *Hello, hello?* the woman had
said, and then, when Elizabeth answered, louder and louder,
Oh! It isn't—he isn't home, is he? Tell him to call Lucinda back. Her
husband had denied knowing a Lucinda, and they had
laughed about it again. And then there was the incident she
had investigated years ago, obviously, but that was just too
embarrassing to think of.

"So you think he might have been having an affair," John
said. His face was purple, as though it had cost him a great
effort to speak so plainly.

"That doesn't seem like something your father would do,
John, but we have to be—well, there's a police investigation,
now, and we have to think that perhaps some things will come
up that neither of us will like."

"Did you know?" John said. "Or suspect this? Once the will was read, maybe? Or before?"

"Slow down, darling, I don't understand you."

"I mean when did you know? Or when did you think you knew? That night, after we all went to bed…" He cut himself off, rising sharply from the sofa. He raised his hands to his head; the half-eaten peanut butter sandwich was still clutched in one of them.

"The will was a surprise," Elizabeth said. "A terrible one. But perhaps your father was trying to—well, maybe atone for his mistakes. Make things right."

John wheeled on her, eyes blazing. "That's what you thought, then?" John said. "Did you speak to Tatiana about it? That night?"

Had she? That night was a blaze of impressions— horrible impressions, each one more scarring than the next. Had she taken time to really talk to Tatiana about it all? To do more than send a shocked look her way, to scour her for any signs of the deceit they all suspected, to smile blandly at her when Tatiana turned, eyes wide and surprised to take in Elizabeth?

"Mom?"

Elizabeth smiled again, a reflex. "I can't remember, darling."

"You can't remember?"

"No. Should I?"

John was looking at her so strangely now, his expression twisted in confusion and something like fear. Had she frightened him? About what?

"When you were walking around that night," John said, and he sounded careful—so careful! "What were you doing?"

What was she doing? Walking, of course, and she had gone to the kitchen…and then there was that nasty little part she didn't want to remember, didn't wish to remember, but she didn't need to burden John with that.

"I don't remember much," Elizabeth said finally. "I'm tired, dear. Shall we put the fire out?"

He still stared at her hungrily, as if he wanted something more. Did he know? Elizabeth wondered. No, of course not, and she wouldn't tell him if she didn't need to. What would be the point? It was all over now.

A buzz cut through the silence. John fumbled with his pockets and pulled out his phone. "It's Michael," he said, frowning.

"Take it," Elizabeth said. "I'll put out the fire." Right after she burned a few more things.

CHAPTER 33

*J*ohn felt sick when he left his house. He had barely been able to focus when Michael was talking to him, telling John that he had something to tell him, asking John to meet him out at the Rhino Bar at the edge of town. Did Michael know? Had he told anyone? Would he be *wired*, for heaven's sake?

John could feel the panic pressing down around him. His mother, a murderess. He couldn't believe it. And yet, and yet! Why was she acting so dreamy, so strange? Why had she looked at him with that dark expression just now, and told him that she couldn't remember?

What was she burning?

He thrust the thoughts out of his mind. Fifteen minutes later he parallel parked a block away from the Rhino Bar. It was a busy night; John could hear the live music playing as he stepped outside. The bar was brightly lit from below, illuminating the beige bricks and white windowsills covered with shriveled poinsettias, as well as the black sign in block print featuring the name of the place with a roughly sketched image of a rhino. It was a boisterous bar, one that John had never much liked, and one he was pretty sure Michael rarely frequented, too. But it had narrow little booths that were well-insulated, and indeed, John found Michael sheltered in one of these at the back. He made his way through a haze of cigar smoke, battling against the smell of whiskey and burnt rosemary.

"Glad you could make it," Michael said solemnly. He tossed John a thin beer menu. "Drink?"

John declined.

Michael was agitated. John could see it in the way that his cousin's fingers drummed against the dark table, in the way that his gaze flitted to the revelers behind them, enjoying the live music (*Bang! Clang! Strummmm*), in the way that he occasionally took long swigs of the beer in front of him, seemingly unable to keep still.

"I wanted to give you a heads-up," Michael said. He winced, then braced himself. "The police have come to see me."

John's stomach flipped, though of course he had thought of this possibility. "And?"

"They asked more of the same. About Tatiana. Your father."

"Okay."

Michael took another swig of his beer. "Sorry," he said, stifling a burp. "This is really uncomfortable."

For you? John thought.

"It's none of my business," Michael continued. "I just wanted to let you know, I didn't tell them anything." He paused. "But I wanted to tell you what I know."

John looked up sharply at Michael. His cousin did look miserable: rings around his eyes, uneven stubble on his chin. He looked like he hadn't gotten a good night's sleep in days. *Probably*, John realized, *just the same as me.*

"Know about what?" John said cautiously.

Michael opened his mouth, closed it. Steeled himself

again. "Tatiana was having an affair with your dad," he said. "I knew her, a little bit. We were friends."

John didn't realize until that moment just how much he was holding on to hope that somehow, everyone had gotten it wrong. That his father, his wonderful, kind, loyal father, had not been capable of such a betrayal.

But he struggled to master himself. "Okay," John said. "Go on."

Michael apologized with each pause as he told the story. He had met Tatiana a couple of years ago, at one of the Eastwick holiday parties. She had been pretty and kind, but aloof, until Michael introduced her to his girlfriend at the time. Then she had opened up: they had enough in common to enjoy each other's company, and Michael got a kick out of hearing her work stories.

They stayed in touch, a little, over the next year or so. Tatiana seemed under the impression, Michael said, blushing, that he was much closer to his uncle than he was. When she mentioned the affair, Michael had been shocked. But Tatiana acted as if it was a known thing, as if Elizabeth Eastwick was both aware of it and approved of it, somehow.

"That's ridiculous," John interrupted. Michael quickly agreed with him.

And yet, Michael said, that was what Tatiana truly seemed to believe—or maybe only what she told herself. Michael realized during this time that he had assessed her incorrectly: he had thought Tatiana engaging and sweet, when really she was calculating and selfish. She was able to convince herself that she loved someone if they could benefit her. She was able to convince herself that having an affair with a married man was justified because (she believed) his wife knew about it, and because they were "really in love."

"I think she thought that your father would leave your mother, eventually," Michael said apologetically, eyes slipping down to his hands. "That's how she talked about it, anyway. That they were waiting for the right time. I'm sorry, John."

"Why are you bothering to tell me this?"

Michael blinked. "I thought you'd want to know. It will come out anyway, in the investigation."

John gritted his teeth. "Fine. You told me. Is that all?"

"Really, John?"

"Really. My apologies, did you expect me to react differently to the revelation that my father was having an affair?"

He watched Michael's lip curl, as much as at his tone, John knew, as at the roundabout, lofty way he had spoken. Still putting up little barriers in his mind. Still hiding the truth with fancy words, when simpler and cruder ones would have done.

"Listen," Michael said. "Screw your feelings. This is about family. And you know that the police are going to go after your mom for this."

John bristled.

"I'm not asking if you know anything, and I don't *want* to know anything. I'm just telling you what type of person Tatiana was, and what we need to do. Heck," Michael said, blowing a strand of hair away from his face, "you don't know the half of it with her. You know that I went to visit your dad's office a couple summers ago? To ask for an internship?"

John had indeed heard the story, or a modified version of it. Michael had shown up early in the morning at his father's office, and Tatiana, for whatever reason, let him wait inside. His parents had remained tight-lipped about why, exactly, they were so angry to find Michael that morning: he assumed because Uncle Edward had sent Michael to ask for money, or because (ha!) Michael and Tatiana were *making out* or doing something equally inappropriate in the office.

"Well," Michael continued, without waiting for John's response. A waiter hovered nearby, saw their animated expressions, and left without taking their order. "Your dad might have let me, you know. Except that Tatiana decided to log into his computer. She had *watched him type his password* enough times to learn it. Creepy enough? And she started pulling up these financial documents. I asked her what she was doing, but she was just so—she was so *proud* of herself, as if she expected me to be impressed that she had access to all of it. She even said, 'You know, it would only be a few key strokes to send a few million dollars my way.' I told her that was embezzlement, and she laughed it off, saying she would never do anything to get caught."

"And I suppose you didn't tell anyone this?"

"No, because then your father barged in, saw what screen was open, and threw me out of his office. He had blocked me in with his car, too, so I had to call my mom to pick me up—I don't think he was in the mood to move it for me. He just assumed that it was my idea to open up his computer. If he had thought about it, how would I have logged in? How would I have known what to search? Anyway," he said, shoulders slumping. "That's who Tatiana was."

"Why didn't you say anything before?"

"Well, isn't it obvious?" Michael said crossly. "Who do you think the prime suspect in the murder is?"

John stared defiantly at him. He wouldn't say it.

"I just wanted to say," Michael said, tensing again, "that I'm trying to help you out. Look—I don't think it was—I'm not saying it was definitely anyone. At all. Because sometimes I think…" Michael seemed to catch himself and drew back. "I think we need to have a united front," he said. "If the police ask us anything about our parents, about where they were that night or what they were doing, we don't say anything. Not if we saw someone walking around, not if we suspect something, not if they complained a few years back about someone or something. Right?"

"I don't need to lie to the police," John said haughtily. "I've nothing to hide."

"I'm sure you don't," Michael said. "This isn't about

hiding the truth. It's just..." He seemed to grow frustrated, facing John's close-lipped expression. John couldn't help it. He wasn't in the mood to bat conspiracy theories back and forth, or act like they were in some sort of newly minted mafia, where they'd keep it all in the family. But he did need allies. And if Michael was suggesting that he knew something about Elizabeth...if he was saying that he saw something and would keep quiet, if John kept *his* parents out of any nonsense, then it was an offer he had to take.

"Never mind," Michael finished, throwing down a ten-dollar bill. "Sorry I asked."

"No, wait. It's not—it's not a bad idea."

Michael paused, searching John's eyes.

"Though I'm not sure what you get out of it," John added, a little testily.

Michael laughed, short and humorless. "Trust me," he said. "Out of the four of our parents, I think mine have just as much, if not more, to hide." He rose again, and John followed him out of the bar. They shook hands as they left, John with a sinking feeling in the pit of his stomach.

CHAPTER 34

*A*nnette was escorted out of the police station late in the evening, when a purple dusk was just settling over the town. "What about Luke?" she had demanded, and the young, wide-eyed woman leading her out had cowered and demurred, until finally she agreed to fetch a superior. Detective Stone came out and assured Annette that Luke would be "finished in a few hours."

"So you're not arresting him," Annette said, hating the sound of hope in her voice. How could she start over, go to Hawaii, when she knew Luke was still dealing with something like this?

"He hasn't been arrested," Detective Stone said. A dodge. So they must still be deciding whether they would. Annette trembled but tried to hold her head high as Detective Stone bid her farewell.

She could have tried demanding to see him again, citing her status as Luke's lawyer. But Annette had the feeling that if she pressed too hard, the police would arrest Luke, make everything more formal, more scrutinized. They might not even let her stay on as his counsel—not that she could, anyway, since if things really got going, Annette was hardly qualified to serve as a criminal defense attorney.

What had he gotten himself into?

Annette left, trying to stem the rising tide of panic in her chest. Normally now was when she would take out her cell phone and call Luke, and if he wasn't available, Mr. Eastwick. Mr. Eastwick always knew how to fix a problem. But her one powerful friend in the world was gone, and her one confidante was currently being interrogated by the police for a crime in which all clues pointed to him. Annette's hands shook as she took out her keys and climbed into her car.

She needed to call someone, though. Aunt Lillian? The idea was laughable. Her aunt didn't even know she was leaving for Hawaii, not yet. John Jr.? Maybe in ten years—but now, he was only a child, still mourning the death of his father.

Elizabeth. She could call Elizabeth. Elizabeth had always been kind to her. She would listen. Annette pulled up the contact on her phone and pressed "call." Her breath shuddered in and out. She pinched her hand to keep from crying, shivering in the cold car in the police parking lot.

"Annette," came Elizabeth Eastwick's soft voice on the other line. "Is everything all right?"

"I'm sorry," Annette said, and found that she couldn't still her voice. It was wobbling uncontrollably; there was no way to hide that she was crying. "I know you're dealing with so much, and I just—"

"Slow down, Annette. You can talk to me."

Annette began to cry. When she had finished, Elizabeth waiting patiently on the other end of the line, she took a deep breath, and began to speak.

CHAPTER 35

"They could have been in on it together," Detective Stone said, sliding into her seat across from Detective Bordeaux. Bordeaux was leaning back in his seat and tossing a hacky sack up in the air, like he was performing some bad impression from a cop show. They were always doing that, Stone thought: acting like the cops they saw on TV, emulating what they thought the police behaved like, because they had to have some model. All of them did it. Once, after a popular TV series called *Silverbadge*, Stone noticed all of her coworkers walking around with a slight lurch, just like the salty (but very attractive) main detective.

She shook herself as Bordeaux answered her. "They could have conspired, but not likely," he said lazily. "They don't act like they're afraid the other one is going to implicate them in something. The lawyer seems mostly scared for him. The chef seems mostly scared."

Stone shrugged. "Should we release him tonight, then?"

"Oh, yeah. Coolidge isn't in, so no point in trying to rush things tonight," Bordeaux said, referencing the prosecuting attorney.

"But we should give him a scare tomorrow. Show him

what we have. That way, if the lawyer *was* in on it, he might think of cutting a deal—"

"She wasn't," Bordeaux said, grinning. He caught the ball a final time and spun towards her. "Want to bet on it?"

"I don't bet."

"Smart girl."

"Stupid boy."

Bordeaux laughed. Stone thought of all of the other evidence they had discovered in the course of the day, all pointing to the Eastwick's chef. Primarily, the fact that Luke Newberry seemed to be packing for a trip—and Annette Jenkins appeared to know nothing about it.

"There's still a chance that they were planning to leave together," Stone said.

"Ha! No chance. She kept talking about moving alone. And she had broken up with him, hadn't she? A bit creepy to follow her out."

"Maybe," Stone said. Something still troubled her. It looked like Luke was getting ready for some sort of move, alright, but he had been so cagey when they had asked him about it. But a search of his apartment had shown bags packed for a trip, and a little more digging had shown that Luke Newberry had already sold his sedan to a woman in Kentucky, who was to pick it up that weekend.

Had he really, then, just planned to steal the million-dollar painting and take flight? Perhaps. Perhaps his mother had contacts with the art world, and Luke knew something about selling on the black market. Or perhaps his prison connections made it possible. It was too bad, Stone thought, for he seemed a nice enough fellow—and hopelessly in love with the lawyer. Maybe that's what made him do it: thinking that if he was rich, he could somehow find his way back to her.

"But why did he bother to steal the painting, after getting the inheritance?" Stone wondered out loud.

"You forget: he probably planned that before the reading

of the will. So once that was read, he had a decision to make —wait to see how much he was getting, or go forward with a foolproof plan." Bordeaux shrugged. "I guess he decided to stick to the original."

"Maybe," Stone said. She tapped her finger on her chin. It still wasn't satisfying...she thought of John Eastwick, pale-faced and frightened that night, of Elizabeth Eastwick, dreamy-eyed and distant, of Luke and Annette, both frightened and defensive in their own way, of Michael, sharp-eyed and defiant, of Vanessa and Edward Eastwick, serpentine and calculating.

"Wait," Stone said, eyes widening. "Bordeaux. I've got it."

CHAPTER 36

*V*anessa was dusting her son's room with a feeling of something like peace. She had called a lawyer, who had reassured her that the funds from her brother-in-law's estate would be quite generous, and that a little loan against their house would tide them over until such time as they could access it. He had even said, with a warm and solicitous tone, that he could help them expedite the process, for an appropriate fee.

Vanessa wasn't a fool. He was a scavenger, out for money, but the fact that made her breast swell with pride was that he was after *her* money. She was a worthy target now. She was rich, or would be.

She hummed as she ran a cloth over her son's bookcases and nightstand. Of course the housekeeper that came twice a week did most of the heavy work, but Vanessa enjoyed playing the role every now and then. Besides, it gave her a fantastic chance to snoop.

Michael kept things fairly neat; he at least drew the comforter back over the pillows of the bed, which was more than she could say of his father. His clothes had been folded over the back of his desk chair, their pockets empty save for the odd coins here and there and a receipt from a gas station two towns over. Vanessa hummed louder. It *was* quite a lovely winter day, the sun bright and cheery outside, the grass covered with a fresh layer of frost, like dusted eyelashes. How beautiful Aspen would be this time of year! She would see Sally Livingsworth, no doubt, and just think of how her face would transform when she heard of Vanessa's good fortune! Sally loved to rub all of *her* great luck in Vanessa's face; Vanessa would oh-so-enjoy the opportunity to return the treatment.

Vanessa paused as her hand slipped inside the pocket of her son's suit jacket, the one he had worn the night of the memorial service. She tugged something out and stood staring at it for some moments before turning it over in her hands.

She blinked. Shook her head.

Impossible.

"Mom?"

Vanessa stuffed her hand back into the suit jacket pocket and swung around, wiping her now-empty hands on her pants. "Just tidying up a bit!" she said as her son's eyes darted suspiciously to his jacket.

Michael shut the door to the bedroom behind him. For some reason, Vanessa tensed. Ridiculous! She wasn't afraid of her son. She wiped her hands on her knees and giggled. The problem was that her body was trying to figure out an appropriate reaction while her mind was working furiously, trying to piece things together.

"I just spoke to John," Michael said. He sat on the edge of his bed and crossed his arms, and just like that he looked like her son again, young and stubborn and vulnerable. "We agreed we'd keep our mouths shut about anything that we saw that night."

"Oh?" Vanessa's heart picked up for an entirely different reason.

"It's for the best. We're family, after all. We have to protect each other."

"Naturally."

He still looked troubled. Vanessa wanted to reach out and brush the lock of hair from his eyes, but Michael always hated when she did that.

"We should always protect each other," Vanessa said carefully. "And I'll protect you forever, Michael. You know that, don't you?"

Michael shrugged, looking away.

"So if there's anything you want to tell me," she said. "Anything at all—you know you can trust me. I'd do anything for you. I'd kill for you." She laughed nervously, a harsh bray. Michael gave her an odd look.

"Is there anything that you want to tell *me*?" he asked, frowning.

"Me! Heavens, Michael, of course not."

"Are you always going to lie to me? Sorry, I should rephrase. Do you really expect me to tell you anything if you keep lying to my face?"

Vanessa's heart stuttered again. She should have reprimanded him, told him that he should never speak to his mother like that. She bet John never spoke to his mother in the same manner. The problem was that she had spoiled Michael: she had loved him so much that she had wanted to shower him with adoration and presents every single day, to bubble-wrap and let him know how wonderful and special and unique he was, to save him from a world that would tear him down and spit him out if she wasn't there to protect him, cocoon him.

"I don't know what you're talking about," Vanessa said.

"We have to stop lying to each other," Michael said. He was looking down at his hands. "This isn't going to work if we keep lying."

"I haven't lied about anything, Michael," Vanessa said nervously.

"I've been trying to protect you. But I can't protect you if you don't—if you keep dodging everything…"

"I'm not dodging anything," Vanessa said. Her voice had gone up an octave.

Michael stared at her. Vanessa stared back. She loved her son, she *would* kill for him, but she wouldn't break over this. What if, she thought, with a pang in her stomach, he was wearing a wire? No, ridiculous. If he was working with the police, they would know—surely he wouldn't have in his pocket that—

"I want to help you," Michael said, frustrated. "Why are you looking at me like that?"

"I have no idea why you think I need help."

He threw his hands up in the air, face red, brows knit. "I don't know why I bother," he muttered, turning to leave the room.

But no sooner was he at the door than Edward appeared, holding a drink in one hand and the TV remote in the other. "Hello!" he said, face ruddy with drink. "I heard some raised voices. Wanted to—ah, excuse me," he said, burping and hitting his chest, "make sure that everything was all right."

He said this with a scathing look at Vanessa. She returned it: if Edward thought she was foolish enough to reveal anything of that night to Michael, he was even more of an idiot than she thought.

"What did you and Mom do the night Tatiana was killed?" Michael said.

Edward blanched. He swirled his drink, the ice cubes clinking against the side of the glass, and looked again at Vanessa.

"Whoa-oh," Edward said finally, raising the hand with the remote. "What are you talking about, son? Seem a little bent out of shape, there."

"Just answer the question."

"What lies has your mother been feeding you?" No doubt he meant it to come out jovial and unconcerned, but his voice dripped with acid. He bestowed another scathing look on his wife.

"I was just telling Mom that I want to help," Michael said tightly, folding his arms, "but I can't do that if you guys are always lying to me."

"Help with what?"

Michael shook his head.

"What have you been saying, eh?" Edward said, turning on Vanessa. His eyes were rimmed with red, and Vanessa noted that he seemed a little wobbly on his feet. "What have you been putting into poor Michael's head?"

"Nothing, you dimwit," Vanessa said. "Go finish your drink."

"I won't have you poisoning my son," Edward said. Yes, he had definitely had more than a few cocktails that night. The idiot would spill more than she ever did, if he wasn't careful.

"Great choice of words," sniffed Vanessa. Michael whipped on her, eyes wide. Vanessa tensed.

"Anything I did, I did for my family!" Edward declared, waving the hand with the remote again.

"Oh, shut up, Edward."

Edward took a menacing step forward, eyes squinting at Vanessa. She just raised one eyebrow. Edward was a coward, a sneak, a mean-spirited, low fool, but he had never struck her, and she was sure he wouldn't start now.

"Yeah, well, you can't say the same, eh?" Edward said. "You ever tell our boy about your last job? The gallery one? You ever tell the *police detectives* about it? Or you think they'll find out on their own?"

"Edward, for heaven's sake!"

Michael's eyes darted between his parents. Vanessa colored. The gallery job had been part-time and short-lived, and she had only taken it because they had been in such dire straits. Not for the hourly pay—that was laughable—but because it gave her the opportunity to network with some well-to-do collectors, who had connections to the finance industry. It had all been to help Edward land another job, though the lazy slob had laughed in her face each time she brought him a card and suggested she invite someone out for coffee, telling her that she was only working there to "procure her next husband."

Well! And if she met a kind, rich gentleman who would care for her more than Edward, what of that?

"I'm sorry, you mean when I was trying to keep our family afloat?" Vanessa said.

"That's one way to look at it, I suppose. Did you tell Michael about the counterfeits?"

Bastard! Hadn't they come up with that idea together? "I have no idea what you're talking about."

"Hmm, really? That young sculpture designer, what was his name—Draco or Drago or something awful like that. He made things out of corks and wires, Michael, and at one show the inventory was running out, and what does your clever mother do? She fashions a few little sculptures of her own, and sells them—out at a show, mind you. The gallery knew nothing of it; Draco certainly didn't; and voilà! She's thousands of dollars richer, and a bunch of rich folks with mush for brains have certified Vanessa Eastwick cork sculptures in their home right now, masquerading as the real thing."

Vanessa's cheeks were burning. She could see the way Michael was looking at her, calculating. "That was years ago," she spat, spinning on Edward. "We were two months behind on our mortgage, and you—you had stopped going out on job interviews."

"Stop," Michael said, voice raw. "I don't want to hear about this."

"See!" Edward cried. "You've upset him."

Her husband and son were both watching her now, both with their bright eyes and long, stern expressions. Ridiculous! she thought. *They* were judging *her*? Whose idea had the crime been that night? What had Michael been up to when she and Edward were carrying out their plans? Why was *she* always the scapegoat, just because the men in their blasted family couldn't face anything wrong they ever did?

"Why were you carrying sleeping pills?" Vanessa said.

Michael went still. "What?"

"Go on, Michael. Be honest with me. You seem to value it. Why did you have sleeping pills in your coat pocket?"

He was silent for a moment. Edward tried to speak. "Vanessa, I don't think—"

"No," Michael said, holding up his hand. "You want to know, Mom? You really want to know?"

Vanessa made a motion for him to continue.

"Because when John was hovering over Tatiana, panicking, I knew that something had happened. And I saw the pill bottle next to the bed. Except what was in that bottle wasn't sleeping pills."

Vanessa frowned. "Well, then?"

"They'd been switched out," Michael said. "The brand didn't even match. Do you know why?"

"Enlighten me."

Michael shook his head. "You know why I took them? Because I thought, in case anyone in the family…. I just wanted to protect you." He shook his head in disgust. "I'm no better than any of you."

"Wait a second," Edward said, his drunk mind whirring to catch up. "You think *Vanessa or I* poisoned Tatiana?"

"Of course we didn't," snapped Vanessa. "And if you want to know who had access to stronger drugs, just look at Elizabeth." Vanessa sniffed. She had kept this particular secret long enough—even the heavy hints of it she had dropped to her husband, over the years, had gone unnoticed. "She had a mental breakdown years ago. Her medicine cabinet is filled with every which thing you can think of."

Michael and Edward exchanged a glance. Vanessa felt something like triumph: soon, she thought, Elizabeth Eastwick would be going down.

CHAPTER 37

*E*lizabeth Eastwick had always had faith in her husband John.

Except, of course, for that one time.

They had been married for three years, and Elizabeth had just been thinking about how it might be getting time for them to start thinking about kids. Oh, John had brought up the idea a half-dozen times over their marriage, but it had always been understood between them that Elizabeth would determine that timeline. And she was ready.

John had been away on a business trip. Elizabeth had been waiting for him the Sunday night of his return; they had lived in a condo downtown, then, in the city, while John's parents were still at the estate. She had made his favorite pasta and left it simmering on the stove, the scent of rosemary and garlic perfuming the air. She had changed into a long silk robe, too (she had always loved them, even then), and lit a candle, humming to herself as she did so and thinking that once they had children, such luxuries would be off limits.

She waited.

An hour passed. Then another hour. Elizabeth had checked the weather, and then debated whether she should call the airport to ask about any flight delays. Was that what one did? She had lived very modestly, before John; she and her family had never traveled much, and she was not sure what the proper protocol was.

Finally, three hours later, the landline rang.

"Hello!" It was John's voice, loud and bright in her ear. She could hear the sounds of laughter and clanging glasses behind him. "Elizabeth! Elizabeth?"

"Yes! Yes, John? It's me!" she shouted into the receiver, looking at it with some perplexity, as if she could see through the phone and into the scene on the other end. "Hello?"

"Hello, darling! Good news! We closed the deal! Marcus wanted to celebrate, so we're actually"—a loud burst of woman's laughter, and another teasing voice, saying her husband's name. It sounded as though he were in a restaurant, or bar. "We're actually going to come home tomorrow!" John said.

Elizabeth heard Marcus' voice in the background, telling him to hang up the phone and finish his drink. She did not wait for more. She hung up.

She waited for him to call back. He had to know she was angry, after that. She stared at the black phone in the kitchen of the condo, arms crossed, eyes darting at the water view of their high-rise, all dark river and sparkling lights.

John did not call.

Elizabeth then went, in plain terms, a little mad.

It would have been better if she had smashed plates and thrown vases. It would have been much simpler had she thrown a tantrum, even opened those high windows the four inches they *would* move and tossed her husband's best suits out into the water. But no. Elizabeth hunkered down, and waited.

For the next few weeks she tracked her husband's movements and calls. She had been so happy, since she had met John: why shouldn't it all be a lie? Why shouldn't he be cheating on her? She had never thought of it before! She kept notes about his mileage at the end of each day. She called his office at random times to check if he was in.

And three weeks later, a break: John had just left the office, the secretary said, and did she want to leave a message? Elizabeth hung up. She sped to the downtown skyscraper, just a few blocks away, and followed John in her car as he wound his way out of the city and to a swanky northern suburb. She parked some distance away from the restaurant hotel that he pulled up at and waited a few beats before following him into said restaurant. She was ready to confront the concierge and demand that he tell her which room her husband had gone into; she was all ready to burst into said hotel room, catching her husband in some compromising position; she was ready to give a movie-worthy demonstration of her rage, and to look scornfully at the woman with whom her husband was committing adultery (the phrase sounded more formal, more serious, and more impressive than mere 'cheating').

Except none of this happened. Elizabeth, after shrieking in the hall for someone to assist her, saw her husband rise from the hotel bar, where he was with one of the clients Elizabeth had met before—Sorry Steve. Sorry Steve was, per his name, always apologizing for this or that, and even as Elizabeth entered the room Steve leapt up from his seat and began to apologize for keeping her husband, and for being in the way, and for not seeing her sooner.

John had held himself pretty well, all things considered. Especially since Elizabeth had had no real explanation for him —she merely said that she had been mistaken about something, and excused herself, embarrassed. She was shaking as she drove away from that parking lot; part of her thought of packing a bag and staying at a hotel for the night, just so she wouldn't have to run into John. They had had a terrible fight that evening, as Elizabeth by turns defended her behavior and cried about it, and John had been alternatively conciliatory and comforting and then frustrated when rebuffed.

It was when Elizabeth's mood only grew blacker in the next few days that John called in professional help. He begged Elizabeth to go to therapy, which she did. Her mother had died just the year before, and that, coupled with a thousand other stresses, had led to what the middle-aged counselor called a "maelstrom of psychological difficulties." John called Vanessa, too, her closest friend at the time, though even then Elizabeth and Vanessa had begun to drift apart. Vanessa was no help: she had rushed over, of course, desperate to see the crisis between the golden couple, and had stroked Elizabeth's hair and whispered vague insinuations about how one *could* never tell with men, that they were *all* cheaters at their heart, before leaving and checking in on Elizabeth only twice more, each time seeming profoundly disappointed that Elizabeth and John indeed had no plans to divorce.

So had ended Elizabeth's one and only time of doubting John: it had ended with her doubting herself. She had understood then that the specters she saw in the world were shadows cast out by treacheries within herself. She had known that of course John could cheat—anyone, indeed, might cheat under certain circumstances. But she had trusted him, because he had proven himself, over and over, to be worthy of that trust.

And now?

Now John was gone.

And Elizabeth no longer trusted herself.

Her phone rang. She saw Annette's number and considered letting it go to voicemail. She did not wish to talk to anyone anymore. She wished she could go to sleep for a thousand years and wake up when all of this nonsense was over.

But, sighing, Elizabeth answered. "Hello, Annette?"

"Elizabeth!" Annette sounded almost breathless. "Where are you?"

"At the house, of course. I've ordered takeout. Pizzas." She paused. "Would you like any?"

"What? No. Listen, Elizabeth, can I come over?"

"Now?"

"Yes, now. I've got to talk to you." Elizabeth heard Annette suck in her breath at the other end of the line. "*I know who stole the painting.*"

Elizabeth heard Annette prattle on about a few other details. Her mind pirouetted around this information: *who stole the painting*. Who, indeed?

But really, Elizabeth could think of one thing only as Annette spoke on: it really didn't matter. Not anymore. Not with something else, something much darker, looming on the horizon.

CHAPTER 38

*J*ohn returned home with his stomach in knots. He had not been able to rest much since his uncomfortable conversation with Michael at the bar. He had always liked Michael, had always felt sorry for his cousin, born as he was to a greedy mother and a cruel father. But perhaps it was John who was to be pitied—perhaps it was John who was being shown mercy.

He hadn't known what to make of Annette's frantic call, either. She had spoken breathlessly about the paintings, and about who had stolen them, directing him to meet her at his house in thirty minutes. "I'm calling everyone," she said. "But I'm not saying exactly why—not yet. Have to get them there, first."

It didn't seem like a good idea, but then, John didn't have the energy to stop her. When he met his mother in the house, she seemed much the same: in a zombie-like trance, willing to be led, offering him slices of pepperoni pizza as she wandered about the house in her bathrobe, long fine hair pulled into a knot at the back of her neck. When Annette came a few minutes later, the lawyer gave Elizabeth Eastwick a nervous once-over and suggested gently that the latter might want to dress herself, as they'd soon have company.

"I've got it, John," Annette had said triumphantly, as Elizabeth went upstairs to follow Annette's advice. She clapped a hand on his shoulder, her eyes gleaming. "I know exactly what happened."

He felt envious of her at that moment—certainly, he wished that he had been as successful in finding out who had killed Tatiana, and restored with it any peace they could in their house. He tried to murmur something encouraging, though to him the mystery of the painting was far from interesting: they had recovered it, after all, no harm done.

Luke showed up shortly after, pale and shaken. He clasped hands with John and barely looked up at Annette, instead taking a seat in the same library room in which their party had heard the will read so recently.

Michael was next. He looked suspicious and surly. "What's this about the change in the will?" he asked John, who feigned ignorance. Michael's parents arrived soon after, obviously fresh off of a fight: Vanessa loudly stated that any reduction in her portion of the estate would need to be taken up with her own lawyer, while Edward declared himself the enemy of anyone trying any "legal hocus pocus," with a pointed look at Annette.

Finally they were all gathered in the library, and Annette walked to the front of the room.

"Thanks for coming," she said, her eyes bright, almost feverish. John had a brief worry that Annette had gone crazy: that the sudden death of John Eastwick, murder of Tatiana, and near-arrest of her friend had thrown her off the cliff of sanity. "I know we all had a lot of questions about what happened the other evening, and I wanted to clear a few things up."

John cast a glance over the rest of the audience. First to his mother, who looked as out of it as she always had these past few days, near to dozing, struggling to pay attention. His stomach twisted. Then there was Uncle Edward, chewing viciously on his mustache, looking angrily at Annette—no change from the usual. Aunt Vanessa, who looked pale and grim-faced, jaw set, ready to interrupt. Michael, hunched behind his parents, arms crossed over himself. Luke, who looked as near as anyone to passing out, from fear or fatigue or both, John didn't know.

"That night," Annette said, "the person who was going to steal the painting planned to do so before the reading of the will."

A shiver seemed to pass over the room. Annette's audience grew quiet.

"They probably assumed that they would be left out of it," Annette continued. "Or not receive their fair share of something. Now, Luke and I didn't expect anything. We were employees. We were surprised to be there. John and Elizabeth owned the painting, so it wasn't them." Her eyes flicked towards John's cousin, aunt, and uncle. "But there were members of the Eastwick family present who probably thought they were going to get less than they deserved— before hearing the will read."

"Excuse me?" Vanessa said darkly, sneering. "What is this? Because if you're lobbing unfounded accusations just to publicly humiliate us—"

"That doesn't prove anything," Michael said angrily. "What are you trying to say?"

Annette gave Michael a look of pity. "It's just motive," she said.

"It's absolute nonsense, that's what it is!" burst Uncle Edward. He had gone severely purple.

"But there's evidence, too," Annette said. "Turns out Luke's fingerprints weren't on the painting."

"Well, naturally he used gloves!" said Uncle Edward. "It was found in *his* car."

Luke swiveled to give Uncle Edward a withering stare. Uncle Edward, for his part, cleared his throat and angled himself slightly away.

"Right," Annette said. "Whoever stole the painting *did* use gloves, because there weren't any fingerprints on the painting at all. There was, however, a piece of hair on the painting."

"It came from Luke's car, then!" Uncle Edward snarled, though he carefully kept his eyes away from the big chef. "This is ridiculous! Go to the police with your insane nonsense! I'll not have you waste my time! Vanessa, come."

Vanessa ignored her husband, her wrathful gaze still locked on Annette. Annette had turned her gaze towards the woman, too, and for a few moments the women looked at each other in tense silence.

"It was your hair," Annette said quietly.

John's head was reeling. How did Annette know? She wasn't the police. Unless they had told her? But why would they compromise their investigation?

"He's driven you sometime before, hasn't he?" Edward said, turning to his wife. "Isn't that true, Vanessa? Somewhere, surely—"

"Oh, shut up, Edward."

Even Elizabeth Eastwick lifted up her head to look curiously at her sister-in-law. Vanessa's mouth was pursed. She was still staring at Annette, open hatred in her eyes.

"That's what the police told me when they released Luke," Annette said softly. "And it makes sense. Luke and I stayed up that night talking in the kitchen. The only people that we saw wandering about were Elizabeth and you two." She indicated Uncle Edward in the sweep of her hand. "You said you were looking for a glass of water, but you were seeing if anyone was still down there, weren't you? And you saw that we were up, but distracted. So you took your chance.

"And then," Annette continued, drawing in a breath, "Tatiana was killed. The police were coming. So you had to hide the painting, but not in your car, in case it was missed. And it was too late to put it back, with everyone wandering through the house. So you got it into the garage, and in Luke's car, which was unlocked."

"Absolute nonsense," Uncle Edward spat. "I'd expect it of you! Conniving lawyer, always think you're cleverer than the rest of us."

"You said it was someone who expected to get nothing in the will," Michael said. His face was pale, almost yellow, and he looked like he was about to be sick. "Why couldn't it have been Tatiana? She couldn't have expected anything."

"Of course, but she was just your uncle's secretary."

"Not just." Michael swallowed and glanced over at Elizabeth Eastwick, who blinked and let her head droop.

Annette blushed. "I don't know about that," she said. "But she didn't steal the painting. She was murdered."

"Maybe she was murdered *because* she was stealing it."

"Wait a second," John said, spinning to Michael. "Are you trying to say my mother or I did it? Because Tatiana was *trying to take a painting?*"

"I'm not saying anything! I'm just saying that Annette's story doesn't make sense," Michael said. "Don't you see? It could just as easily have been Tatiana. It could have been any of us—including Annette." He frowned up at her. "Pretty trick, inviting us all here and making some sort of big claim based on flimsy evidence."

"Evidence strong enough that the police released Luke," Annette said. "Evidence strong enough that the police have put a hold on Edward and Vanessa Eastwick's passports in the interim."

"Excuse me!" Uncle Edward shouted.

"Passports!" Vanessa cried. "That's unacceptable—unacceptable!" She colored and turned to her husband. "*Do something!*"

Uncle Edward rose, arms flapping uselessly, and looked

about him. Realizing there was no one nearby whose neck he could wring, or anyone standing who he could menace with his fists, he sat promptly back down.

"What if Tatiana spotted the thief?" John said, looking at Annette. "If they thought they'd been discovered—"

"So you're saying my parents stole the painting *and* killed Tatiana?" Michael shouted behind him. The two cousins rose, eyes sparking. John felt the weight of their parents' potential sins between them, their tentative truce close to going up in flames: John would protect his mother at all costs, and Michael would do the same for his parents. If the painting thieves had been discovered by Tatiana, and had murdered her…he could barely admit to himself how much he hoped in this outcome, how much he hoped beyond hope that his mother had nothing to do with any of it.

"I don't care about the painting," Elizabeth murmured, almost to herself. "I don't care…I wouldn't care…"

"Wait!" Vanessa cried. Her eyes lit up. She swiveled first towards her husband, and then towards Annette. "The painting is part of the estate."

Annette blinked.

"So no one here could have stolen it!" Vanessa said, clapping her hands together. "It's not stealing! *It's all ours.*"

"That's not quite how it works," Annette said coldly.

"We can't legally be held liable for something like that," Vanessa said, turning towards her husband. He looked at her dubiously. "It's all ours! We're inheriting it! Who cares who has what part of the property now? It all has to be divided up in—in probate, right?"

"Mom," Michael said.

But Vanessa was beaming now, delighted with herself. "It doesn't matter if the police found my hair in Luke's car," she said, sniffing. "It was *my* painting to take. And why not? We're equal inheritors of the estate, after all."

"Allegedly," Edward added quickly. "Allegedly, she took it."

"You're not talking to the police," John said, rolling his eyes.

"*Allegedly*," Vanessa said sweetly, smiling up at Annette with venom. "*Allegedly*, yes, Edward and I decided that we should have the painting, and why not? His brother didn't deserve the whole estate. He was given it by his father, and Edward had been cut out, almost since youth! What if we evened the scales a little by taking the painting? We had as much right to it as anybody. But of course," Vanessa said, lips curling even further, "John had some sort of fever before he died, obviously, for he did one right thing in his life and divided the will evenly between us. In which case, why not take the painting?"

"I'm assuming you meant to hide it from the estate, and keep it for yourselves," Annette said, voice still frosty. "The police found the decoy picture in a back storage room."

"Anyone could have put that there," Edward said.

"Who knows?" Vanessa replied, examining her manicure. "Doesn't matter, not now. We never did take it, did we? Only moved it."

John was staring aghast at his aunt and uncle. He had never gotten along with them, it was true. He had always felt awkward around them, always felt their resentment as a palpable force behind their fake smiles and polite questions about how he was, and how he was liking that private school or that expensive family trip. But this sort of open hostility, the *hatred* emanating from his aunt, he had never guessed at before.

Was it enough to lead to murder?

What if, indeed, his aunt had wanted more than just an eighth of the estate? Because with Tatiana dead, everyone's share would increase. Indeed, what if she and John's uncle had intended to target even more people that night...?

His mind spun. He couldn't tell if it was wishful thinking

on his part to believe his mother innocent, or if he really was onto something.

"So you admit it," Annette said coolly. "You took the painting."

"Moved it to Luke's car. What of it?" Vanessa said. "Edward and I did. And we would have had a right to it, too. But c'est la vie. We'll get our money, one way or another."

Annette breathed a deep sigh. She glanced at Luke, who was staring at her with an inscrutable expression. Finally he rose, and with slow, painstaking steps, made his way into the kitchen. Annette hesitated, then followed.

"This is ridiculous," Michael said, into the uncomfortable silence that followed. John realized that only Eastwicks were left in the room and shuddered. "What a farce!"

"The painting doesn't matter," Vanessa sniffed. She seemed well-pleased with herself. "They should focus on who murdered that poor girl."

"Vanessa," Edward growled.

"What? I liked her well enough. She was the one who told us how valuable it was, back at the Christmas party." Vanessa sniffed. "Didn't she say that, Michael? Worth a fortune, she said. Art history major. Very *refined* young woman—pity."

Michael colored. "Just stop talking about the painting, Mom."

"I'm not. I'm talking about the secretary, that Tatiana girl. She was always so nice to you, wasn't she? And Edward, too; she agreed with me when I said once that it wasn't fair, the way the brothers had been treated. She knew an injustice when she saw one. Though," she added darkly, "I can't say I approve of her taste in men."

"She wouldn't have ever gone for Uncle John," Michael said, with a quick glance at John. "That is—I'm sure there were, um, *unusual circumstances.*"

"What, like he forced himself on her?" John said, rising.

He felt another stab of rage and guilt when his mother started in front of him, bringing her blinking gaze up to his.

"Of course not!" Michael said, mortified. "Let's just—let's drop it."

John fumed. His aunt and uncle had been prepared to steal hundreds of thousands of dollars from them, if not more, and they had to take it because somehow the plot had been foiled, and besides, Uncle Edward and Aunt Vanessa were to inherit part of the estate anyway. It was cruel, too cruel. All of it was.

It wasn't fair. Nothing had been fair since his father's death. John didn't know what to think of himself, because his image of his mother and his father had been so irrevocably shattered. What had happened to the supportive, kind nuclear family that he had known? What had happened to the image of the family he had once had?

Why couldn't he go back to it?

As his mind was whirring, another thought jumped into his head. It was the way that Michael had said something, just now. The conviction in his voice. He blinked. No, that couldn't be right...it was impossible, really. Inconceivable.

John started and turned to his mother.

CHAPTER 39

*A*nnette followed Luke into the kitchen. The chef looked exhausted, wrung through the ringer. His face sagged with fatigue.

"Thank you," he said quietly, taking his familiar perch on one of the kitchen stools. "I don't want to leave with the reputation of a thief."

Annette blinked. "Leave?"

Luke held Annette's gaze for a few beats. She struggled not to let her eyes wander over the lines of his face: the chiseled jaw, the strong and slightly crooked nose, the bright eyes with pale lashes, and the tiny divot at one corner where he had scratched off a chicken pox sore when he was a child. She had missed him so much, she thought. She had been so hellbent on saving him that it had let her push all other thoughts from her mind. Thoughts of her leaving, of Luke staying behind.

"I'm quitting," Luke said quietly. "I'm not going to stay with the Eastwicks any longer."

"Why? Not because of what happened, is it? They're a good family, even if—"

"Not because of what happened."

Annette paled. "Then why?"

"You know why."

Her gaze dropped to his wrists. Strong wrists, with callused hands covered in burns and scars, from where hot pans and sharp knives had sliced his skin. He was a hard worker; it was one of the traits she admired most in him. It was one of the traits that Annette felt sure would make him a good father.

She pushed the thought from her mind.

"I don't know," she said. "Are you okay, Luke? Is everything okay?"

Luke took a long, slow breath. "I'm fine," he said finally. "I'm going to be fine. Don't you worry about me." He rapped the table, as if calling the end to their meeting. "Thanks for everything you did today."

"I bluffed about the hair." She blurted it out, mostly to keep him there longer.

Luke's face broke into the shadow of a grin, which quickly faded. "Yeah," he said, "I guessed."

"Wait," Annette said, as Luke made to rise. "Where are you going? Did you get a new job?"

"Does it matter?"

"Tell me that, at least. So I know you're okay."

Luke's mouth set in a grim line, but he lowered himself back down. "Haven't decided yet. I have a buddy who told me to call him, if I ever needed work. I might travel for a bit, then settle down there when I need to."

"Where? Where is he?"

"Gloucestershire. Out on the east coast."

It shouldn't have upset her; she was moving to *Hawaii*, after all, and it wasn't like Luke could move much further from where she had decided to go to. And besides, it wasn't like she had a claim on him anymore: he could go where he pleased, do what he pleased.

But why did it have to be that way?

"Gloucestershire," Annette said, biting her lip. An image

flashed into her mind: her and Luke, strolling through lush trees and across steep mountains in Hawaii, pausing to admire turquoise blue water, Luke's hand around her waist and the scent of dirt and flowers assailing them. She had never asked him because she had never wanted him to know just how desperately she needed to leave. She had never asked him because it seemed too much too soon, when they had known each other for so little time. She had never asked him because he had a great job, a plum job, and who was she to take away someone else's dream just because she found that hers was not all it was cracked up to be?

"Are you…are you sure?" Annette asked.

There was something in Luke's gaze as his eyes snapped up to her. Something almost hungry, electric. He searched her face, and it was all she could do not to look away, to cower from something so bright and naked and vulnerable.

"Do you want me to go?"

Annette sucked in her breath.

"Say the word, and I'll come with you. But if you don't, you won't hear from me again. I won't bother you." His jaw was getting more rigid, expression more closed, the longer that Annette held her silence. But she felt as though she couldn't speak; the air had whooshed out of her lungs, and she struggled for a breath.

"I'm not as educated as you," he said stubbornly. "But I work hard, and I can make a good living. I have money saved. I can pull my weight and then some. And I'd help out, too, whatever we needed—I'm good with my hands. I can renovate."

A tear spilled down Annette's cheek. Luke saw it and broke off suddenly, rising. "Well, then," he said, voice strained. "I think I've made a fool of myself enough for the night. Thanks, Ms. Jenkins. I won't forget what you've done for me."

"Luke, hold on." She grabbed his arm and squeezed. She

was powerless to hold him there, but at her touch the big man froze, swiveling slowly towards her. "It's not that. It's just—"

"Just what?"

Luke was staring at her, waiting for an answer. Now was when Annette could tell him: *it's me, not you, and I'm sorry.* Or: *I don't know what I want for myself in life, except some peace, and I don't see where you fit into it.* Or closer to the truth: *I'm afraid, and I'm afraid especially to bring someone I love into my uncertainty, to drown us both.*

But she would be selfish tonight. She would seize the moment because it was the last one she would have.

"Will you marry me?"

The words were out of her lips before she could hold them back. She stood for a moment, mortified, waiting to read anything beyond the shock that registered in Luke's face as he heard her.

Annette clapped her hands to her mouth.

"Wait," Annette said, "don't answer! Look, Luke, I-I should have said something earlier. I should have been honest. I think that I might—that is, I haven't taken a test yet, but…" She swallowed hard. She had been afraid to, because if she did take one, she would be forced to act, and Annette hadn't been ready for that. But she would be lying to herself if she didn't admit that one of the reasons she had chosen Hawaii was that, if she was going to raise a child, that child would be as far from St. Clair and its pernicious influences as she could get it.

"I might be pregnant," Annette finished in a whisper.

Luke didn't answer her. Instead he swept her into his arms, thick and warm, and pressed her close. "I don't care if you are or not," he said. "That is—if you are, I'm happy, but yes—either way, yes!"

Another thought flashed into her head. They hadn't been dating this whole time in one uninterrupted stretch. "Oh,

God," she said. "Luke—you know that if I am, the baby could only be—it would only be *yours*?"

"Oh!" Luke said, blushing, which made it very clear that he did not, in fact, take that for granted. He smiled sheepishly. "Well, that's, uh—that's good to hear, I suppose." She punched him in the arm, and Luke's smile broke out into a full grin.

"I didn't get you a ring," Annette said.

"That's okay. I have one."

"Oh, really?"

"Yup. Bought it on our third date. Was waiting until a good opportunity presented itself."

Annette grinned. Luke pulled her in closer. Something within Annette released, and she felt relief and warmth like she had never known. She would have been fine on her own— she was prepared to be alone.

But having Luke around…that wasn't too bad.

In fact, it was perfect.

CHAPTER 40

*J*ohn followed Michael out of the library, into the living room where the naked patch of wall still advertised the *Stormwood* painting's recent almost-theft.

"Hold up," John said, catching up to his cousin. Uncle Edward and Aunt Vanessa were ahead of them and made their way into the garage even as Michael hesitated, turning back towards John. Elizabeth was still in the library, too languid to move. "I have a question."

"Yes?" Michael said, a little impatiently.

"You said that Tatiana would never go for someone like my dad. What did you mean?"

Michael rolled his eyes. "Look, it wasn't an insult about your dad. Things were just heated. Sorry."

He turned to leave again, but John moved in front of him, blocking his exit. "Yes, but you made it sound like you knew something. Like you were sure Tatiana wasn't interested in him." John paused. "Like she hadn't been having an affair with him."

"I already told you that she was."

"Were you lying?"

Michael's nostrils flared. "I really don't want to keep talking about your family," Michael said stiffly. "I thought we agreed that we were going to move beyond that."

"Were you lying?"

"No!"

They stood in a stand-off for some seconds, Michael's face red and blotchy. John could feel his cousin assessing his own expression even as he did the same, looking for weak points and vulnerabilities.

"If Tatiana wouldn't go for someone like my father," John said slowly, "who would she go for?"

Michael turned an even darker shade of crimson.

"Ah," John said. "Of course—you."

"How ridiculous!" Michael said, tossing up his arms. This time he pushed past John, heedless of his cousin's attempts to thwart him. "You really need to get your head checked, cousin. Sorry that your parents aren't all they're cracked up to be, but if you haven't noticed, mine aren't either."

"Now hold up. Just talk this through with me," John said. "If the police come and ask—"

Michael whipped back to John. "And ask about us? What? Were you going to say that you'd tell them something about me and her? Are you *blackmailing* me? Because if you are—"

"I'm not. I just want to understand the truth. What you guys were to each other."

"Friends, I told you that."

"But you were romantic, weren't you? Even just for a little bit?"

"I feel sorry for you," Michael said. "I really do. At least I can face what my parents are. You—you aren't able to. You keep making up stories in your head to redeem them, because you can't handle the truth."

"And you're avoiding it," John said, voice catching. He felt his heart rate pick up. John had never struck someone before, but he felt that if his cousin uttered another word about his father, he'd get as close as he'd ever come. "You know that Tatiana and my father never had an affair. You were trying to distract me. By maligning my dead father."

"John with the big words again," Michael said savagely. "Did you learn that at Montvale? Before they kicked you out?"

John held himself back, barely—and only because he knew Michael was baiting him. "Tatiana never had an affair with my dad," he repeated again. "But she did have a relationship with you."

Michael laughed, long and loud. John heard his mother rustling in the other room. "It's sad, really," he said. "You've gone off the deep end."

"You weren't friends. You were dating. That's why she was hiding it from everyone—that's the romance she was talking about. You kept it under wraps. Were you ashamed of her? Or was she ashamed of you?"

Michael moved with a rapidity that caught John off guard. They both went down, legs kicking, arms swinging. John felt a rush of adrenaline, not unpleasant, and some animal part of him thought *yes, now we finally get to have it out....* He wanted to hurt Michael, and be hurt. He wanted to drown out all of his other pain.

But no sooner had they tumbled to the floor than Michael miraculously lifted away from John. After another moment, John saw that the lifting away was not so miraculous after all —instead, Michael was held in the wiry arms of Detective Bordeaux.

"I'll let you go if you calm down," Bordeaux said. Michael squirmed and stomped a few seconds more before falling limp in the detective's arms.

"It wouldn't have ended like this," Michael said. He collapsed now, held up under the strength of Bordeaux's grip.

"It shouldn't have come to this. But your dad had to go and die, didn't he?"

"Let's sit down," Bordeaux said. John was still reeling, trying to process how the detective had gotten into the house in the first place. "We can all have a chat, can't we?"

CHAPTER 41

*I*t turned out that Annette had called Detective Bordeaux and Detective Stone there, stating she had made a breakthrough in the case of the almost-stolen painting. Bordeaux and Stone took their time, of course—it turned out that they had been so interested in the stolen painting because they had assumed, from the start, that whoever had been stealing it had been surprised by Tatiana and had murdered her for witnessing it.

Indeed, by the time they arrived at the Eastwick mansion, Annette's showmanship was over, Uncle Edward and Aunt Vanessa had gone down to the wine cellar to make further use of their new estate, and Luke and Annette were "ah, canoodling," Bordeaux said, rubbing the back of his neck, in the kitchen. Bordeaux had spotted the fight between Michael and John just in time to separate them.

Now Bordeaux had led John and Michael into one of the upper bedrooms, where they were joined by John's mother and Detective Stone. John tried to read something in his mother's expression—resignation, or disappointment, or anger. But she only looked quizzically at him as she perched on one of the arms of the patterned sofa, waiting.

"Now," Bordeaux said, looking between Michael and John, "do you two want to tell me what that was about?"

John looked blankly at the detective and turned to Michael. Michael's face was a mottled red and purple, but he held his chin defiantly up at the detective and remained silent.

"Michael," Detective Stone said. "Maybe you can start."

He jumped at her address. "M-me? Why?"

Stone held his gaze for a few beats. "I think my partner and I are particularly interested in some text and email messages between you and Tatiana Orlov."

John blanched. He glanced at Michael, and then at his mother, who had gone similarly pale. It was true, then? He had taken a wild stab in the dark—intuition, foolishness, whatever it may have been—and had landed on the truth?

Michael's mouth worked. John waited for the inevitable *I want a lawyer*, but Michael was looking between the two detectives now, calculating.

"It wasn't what you think," he said.

Bordeaux nodded so deeply that it was almost a bow. "Tell us," Stone said.

"We met at a party a few years ago," Michael said. His first words came out as a mere mumble, but he seemed to gain strength as he talked. "I didn't even know who she was. She's older than me, and—and, I wasn't going to talk to her, except she came up behind me and started talking about some of the artwork in the mansion. This mansion. *Not* the *Stormwood* piece," he said blushing. "She just seemed genuinely really impressed with everything there. And yeah, it kind of annoyed me. I mean, the only reason that the whole mansion is so impressive is because it's been in the family for hundreds of years. And the family doesn't split anything fairly, ever."

John exchanged a glance with his mother. He had expected this from his aunt and uncle, but he hadn't realized that the resentment had gone so deep—that Michael had been infected, too. He should have realized. He should have asked, should have thought more of his cousin and less of himself.

"So I just started talking about some of the Eastwick history, and we got to talking, and she found out that I was an Eastwick, too." His voice vacillated between pride and embarrassment. "*She* was the one who pursued *me*. She told me that she worked for Uncle John, and that he could be stuck up sometimes, really nice in that way that people are when they think they're so much better than you. No offense," he added to John, who did everything he could in his power to remain absolutely still. "I told her about my family and stuff. She was just—she listened, and she seemed to get it all. You don't meet a lot of people who have any experience with Eastwick royalty and have anything to say other than how envious they are of them."

"You clicked," Bordeaux suggested.

"Well, that's what I said, isn't it? We clicked. And she was really smart—she knew all of this stuff about art and TV, and she even painted a little bit. She said she could show me some of the paintings sometime, but that I'd have to take her out first." Michael exhaled. "I was young, then. I'd barely had a girlfriend before. So I kind of needed that signal to get it."

"And you took her out?" Stone said.

"Well, yeah. This was at the Christmas party, when we met. We said we'd go out New Year's Eve."

"Big night."

"She suggested it. I think she knew that. Girls know that, usually. I made reservations and everything, spent way more than I could afford, and—well. That was kind of how it started."

"You were a couple since that night?"

Michael blushed. "*Couple* is a strong word. That is—I don't know." He seemed to deflate, collapsing in on himself. "It wasn't supposed to go this way," he whispered again, almost to himself. "It didn't have to."

"She was persistent, yeah?" Bordeaux said, exchanging a meaningful glance with Stone. "She had her sights set on you."

"I didn't know anything about being in a relationship, not properly, not right out of college. We went out a few times, and then I kind of just fell off of texting her.... I figured it had come to an end, or whatever. Except she kept calling me. Asking me to meet her places. Once she said she was at the hospital, but when I called her on my way over she said she was fine, and had gone home, that it was just a sprained wrist." Michael shook his head. "And it was *flattering*, you know? Here's this beautiful older woman, really smart, who seems to *like* you, and, and..."

"And you didn't know how to shut it off," Bordeaux offered.

"No. And part of me—I mean, I didn't know what I wanted. I was so young. And she made it really easy, and then we got along so well, and...well. I guess we were official, if you want to call it that."

"But not public."

"It wasn't a good idea. Things have always been tense between my dad and Uncle John. No need for him to find out that his secretary was dating me."

"Really?" Bordeaux said, scratching his chin. "See, me, I wouldn't think that's such a big deal."

"You didn't know my uncle," Michael said darkly. John felt a twinge in his chest. "He would have found a reason to fire her, eventually. He'd think that I was whispering poison about him in her ear, trying to corrupt her or something. Uncle John never liked me."

"That's not true!" John broke out, then clamped his mouth shut. Michael turned his flat gaze on him.

"I'm sure you think so," Michael said. "But he didn't. My dad asked him a half a dozen times to give me an internship at his company. To write a recommendation, make an introduction, do *something*. And he wouldn't. Not ever."

John glanced towards his mother, who shook her head slightly. Michael noticed it.

"What?" Michael demanded. "Aunt Elizabeth, you know it's true!"

"He did make introductions for you," she said softly. "To accounting firms in the city, and in town. To coaches back when you thought you might want to play tennis. But your father…Edward was asking for recommendations for things that didn't make sense for a boy of your age—that he would never have even recommended John for."

"And yet, he's perfectly fine bribing John's way into the best college in the country," Michael snorted. Elizabeth colored, and faded back against the couch. John wanted to spring up and wrap his arms around his mother, protect her not just from Michael's words, but from any negative thoughts about the late John Eastwick Sr. To protect himself, too.

"We *both* agreed it would be better to keep it a secret," Michael said, appealing now to Bordeaux. "Tatiana knew my Uncle John. She agreed."

"And you never told anyone?" Bordeaux said.

"Why would we? At a certain point, when we talked about it, we just said that we would wait until she changed jobs. And then a year passed, and another, and…well. It was just easier not to say anything."

"My dad found you at the office," John blurted. "With Tatiana, one morning. He must have known then."

Michael scoffed. "Your dad would never think highly enough of me to ever even *conceive* of the idea that a woman would want me," he said. "He threw me out that day because he didn't like me, plain and simple."

"That's the thing," Bordeaux said. "There's a few texts from you and Tatiana about a year back…a little strange, referencing that morning. Makes it sound like your uncle caught you two doing something you shouldn't have."

John blushed, his mind immediately jumping to some carnal conclusion. But Michael shifted uneasily. "He jumped to conclusions," he said stiffly. "Tatiana was just showing me some of the company software."

"With confidential financial information?" Bordeaux said. "In John's office?"

"Look, it wasn't my idea," Michael said, coloring. "I told her we shouldn't be in there. But she was...well, to be frank, she was pressing me about making things serious. And I kept telling her that I didn't have the money. That I wasn't one of those rich Eastwicks who could do whatever they wanted in life because I had a huge safety net. She was just joking—she said that a few numbers from that page would set us up for life. *But she didn't mean it*," he said quickly, seeing Bordeaux and Stone's expressions. "Really! Look, Tatiana talked about that stuff, but she never even lied on her timesheet. She was just messing around. Trying to cheer me up."

"Why were you down?"

"I don't remember."

"Really?"

"I don't. Really. Probably some combination of my messed up family, my dead-end career, and my overall cluster of a life," Michael said, with more venom than John had ever suspected his cousin carried in his breast. "Okay? I don't remember. She was just trying to cheer me up, and then Uncle John came in, and of course assumed the worst, and assumed it was *my fault*."

John shuddered. He wondered how, in all of the intervening years, he had missed this so completely. He had seen Michael at Christmas gatherings, at Easter brunches, at the occasional summer event downtown. He had always assumed that Michael was happy, or near enough so; Michael had always been hardworking and humble, in comparison to the parents who had raised him. He had always been kind to John, not overly friendly, but polite and warm. John had looked up to him.

"And did you break up, then?" Stone said. "Seems like it would cause a lot of stress."

"I suggested it," Michael said, letting out a breath. "But Tatiana didn't want to. We just...we kind of just saw each other less. I think she realized I was a lot more dead-end than she hoped I would be."

"Dead-end?"

"Yeah. That I'd never make the real money she wanted. Anyway. We didn't talk about it. I just stopped texting her as much, and she stopped texting me, too. We hadn't spoken in months when Uncle John died."

"And then you reached out? Or she did?"

"She did. I-I went over to her place. She was freaking out, wondering if he had known it was coming. Because he had changed his will recently, in the past few weeks." Michael paused. John and Elizabeth exchanged a wide-eyed stare. "She showed it to me."

"How did Tatiana have a copy?" Stone said, frowning.

"She made one. When he wasn't looking. She knew I— well, we'd talked about it before. How he wasn't going to leave anything to my family, even though he inherited most of it from *his* parents, who expected him to take care of my dad."

"But then you found that it was actually quite generous. *Very* generous."

Michael blushed. "Maybe to everyone else," he snapped. "Not to me. Not to me and not to my family." Michael took a deep breath. John felt as though his chest had constricted. His breath was shallow and short. "He gave these enormous lump sums to his chef and his lawyer and to his employees, and Tatiana got a little something, nothing compared to Poppy and Tyrone—the two people who work for John," Michael explained to the detectives, who nodded. "And then a whole bunch to charity, and the lion's share to his wife and kid, and then a restricted trust to my family, to pass to me after my parents died."

"What's wrong with that?"

"It's an insult! First, why give everyone else lump sums, and act like you have to portion it out to my family? Like you can't give it to us all at once, or *oh no*, we might overspend! And then the amount, too—twenty thousand a year for forty years. How is a family supposed to live off of that!"

"That's over three quarters of a million dollars," Stone said.

"And doesn't sound like so much when you break it down like that, does it?" Michael said. He sucked in a breath. "Look, I know it sounds ungrateful. But *he could have given more*. He had all the money in the world. He could have made us comfortable for the rest of our lives with no skin off his back. But again, he didn't. He chose to donate two million dollars to his alma mater, did you know that?"

John's ears burned. Somehow, growing up, he had been blissfully unaware of matters of family money and wills and trusts. He had never thought about what it would be like when his father passed, when vultures circled and all of his father's money decisions would be held up to the light, examined to search for character flaws. And was it a character flaw, to give more to a college institution than to his flesh-and-blood brother? John couldn't help but feel that some injustice had been done—and yet at heart he hated the money that made his cousin's eyes roll, that made his aunt and his uncle despise his family with a passion, that made every interaction they had fraught with tension, because at stake was not just love and trust but *money*.

"But you don't know anything about my will," Elizabeth

said, voice shaking. "Michael, most of the estate was supposed to pass to me. John had a separate will so that, when he died, he could distribute some of the estate to the people he loved, but most of it won't come until after I pass—"

"It's fine, Aunt Elizabeth," Michael said, blushing. He didn't even lift his eyes to address his aunt. "I'm just telling what happened. Tatiana showed me the will, and—and I said what would really be fair was if he divided it equally. I saw how much it was worth. It would make all of us rich, and he didn't need—"

"But he still had a widow," John said incredulously. "You wanted my mom out of the house?"

"And that just shows how insulated you are from the real world," Michael snapped. "You think even a tenth of your dad's estate is this house? News flash: he has other properties. Investments. Assets. Your mom could have kept the house just fine."

John wanted to argue. Not based on what Annette had said...at the very least, it would have caused an untold number of problems, as lawyers worked out just what everything was worth and who got what. But he kept his lips clamped shut, and Michael kept talking.

"Tatiana said that was a good idea, and that John would even do something like that, if he wasn't so"—a quick glance at Elizabeth—"so controlled by his family. She said she knew where the will was kept in the office. And she said she was a good mimic of handwriting—showed me how she could reproduce the witness signatures."

"So it was Tatiana's idea?" Bordeaux said. "To change the will?"

"We were just joking around, at first," Michael said. "I left and we didn't do anything. But then I started thinking about it...and I thought, why not? Why not help out some people that I loved? It wouldn't hurt anyone. It was *fair*, how it should have been. And I didn't just give it to my family—I gave it to Annette, Luke, Tatiana. All people that were in Uncle John's will in the first place."

"But not your uncle's employees?"

Michael colored. "Look, to be honest, I didn't even want to include Tatiana. Annette and Luke were like family to Uncle John. It would look weird to have employees with an equal share. But she was the one who had to make the switch, right? So I needed her help. And she wanted an equal share. I told her it was stupid, but there you go. And you know what? It didn't even make her happy. We fought more in the next couple of weeks than anytime before. She started to feel guilty, say that it was a joke that had gone too far.

"And then the funeral came, and she really started freaking out. She said she wished she hadn't been in it at all. I kept telling her, *you were the one who wanted to be named in it in the first place!*" Michael took a deep breath. "She kept freaking out. I started ignoring her calls, because I couldn't…there just wasn't any talking to her. And then she told me, the night of the wake, that she was going to confess that the will was wrong. She said it was my fault, that if I hadn't forced her to switch it, we wouldn't be here. She was hysterical. I went to talk to her that night, to calm her down. She took some sleeping pills before I got there, she must have. She was so quiet…she kept telling me it didn't matter anymore. And, and…" Michael buried his face in his hands.

John watched his cousin, his whole body gone cold. Was Michael trying to say that Tatiana, in a fit of guilt, had killed herself?

"But you weren't there when I found her," John blurted. "I found her dead, and, and—you were the first to get there."

"She was sleeping when I left her," Michael said. "I didn't kill her."

Stone and Bordeaux exchanged a glance. "Sounds like she was pretty troubled," Stone said, and even though her tone was even, and she held Michael's hopeful gaze with a steely one of her own, John could tell that she didn't believe it. That she knew. "Did she tell you she took all of those pills?"

"No, I mean…when John found her, I saw the pill bottle, and I took it, because—well, I didn't want everyone to know what had happened."

"That she had killed herself?"

"Yes."

"So you preferred it looked like she had died—naturally—during the night?"

Michael blushed again. He seemed to be struggling with himself, mouth gaping open and then closed like a fish.

"It's okay," Stone said, not unkindly. "You can tell us."

"I was only trying to help!" burst Michael. "I gave her a few…she must have taken some more before I got there…she was crying so much, and she wouldn't be quiet…I didn't mean for her to die!"

And he broke down in wrenching sobs that tore through his whole body. This, John thought mournfully, was nearer to the truth. Nearer, but not quite there yet. He pictured Michael, pleading with Tatiana, begging her not to say anything. Michael, forcing Tatiana to take a few sleeping pills, promising her anything and everything if she would just go to sleep, so they would talk about it tomorrow. Michael, forcing more down her throat when she was asleep, waiting until her breath slowed, waiting until his work was done, and then creeping back to his room to wait. He had coming running when John had discovered her, had realized he had forgotten the bottle of pills and snatched them, as a guilty man would…. Michael, who had been so close to the money he felt he was owed, who had wanted to rid himself of the woman who had been to him a barnacle for so many years, who threatened to undo the very scheme she herself had helped to plot.

"It's okay, son," Bordeaux said solemnly. "We'll go down to the station, hmm? Get this sorted out."

It was strange, but John almost thought he spotted relief in Michael's face as he rose and was ushered out of the room by the two detectives.

CHAPTER 42

a day later, Michael was arrested.

Aunt Vanessa and Uncle Edward were hysterical. They called it a conspiracy. They threatened to sue. They raged at the fact that John and Elizabeth had been in the room "pressuring poor Michael into a false confession," and glossed over the fact that, at the same time, they had been in the wine cellar enjoying the most expensive bottles of the late John Eastwick Sr.'s collection.

Annette went down to the station and offered to help as much as she could. She referred Michael to a criminal defense attorney, whom his parents promptly dismissed as "incompetent," hiring instead a young law school graduate with slicked-back oiled hair and bold pronouncements like, "We'll have him free and clear in two weeks!" Michael dismissed him; he entered a plea.

Tatiana's family came to bury their daughter. Michael requested to meet with them; they refused. Elizabeth paid the funeral expenses. The family, dry-eyed and bright-haired, spoke very little during their visit and left with long faces and somber demeanors.

Poppy and Tyrone were able to find the one copy of the

will that Tatiana had not managed to switch—the copy confirmed by experts to contain the real, unforged signatures of John Eastwick Sr. and his witnesses. The changes made to it were extremely minor, little updates that John Eastwick Sr. had made each year, mostly about real estate properties and charities. The police took the will into evidence; the prior one was voided, and the new lawyer taking over for Annette reassured John and Elizabeth Eastwick that "all would be resolved shortly—probably within one to three years."

Annette and Luke used the generous lump sum eventually given to each of them to help their move to Hawaii—and to help fashion their new baby nursery. They got married quietly on the beach, with no fanfare. Luke soon took a job as a chef at a nearby resort, and Annette opened up an online shop where she offered legal advice and contract templates to clients around the globe. She promised her Aunt Lillian to visit her one day, though she was rather cagey on the timeline. When she stepped outside of their small home and looked out at the mountains and bright sky, her new baby on her shoulder, she wondered to herself that this life could be part of the same one where she had, just months before, suffered so greatly.

The trust set up for Edward and Vanessa Eastwick was a cause of great consternation for the couple. It was, quite plainly to them, not enough money. They had already spent a significant portion of their projected inheritance. And they were victims, they cried, victims of the false will. Surely there was a legal loophole there?

There was not; Michael was scheduled for sentencing, and worse, the Aspen trip was canceled.

John spent the next few weeks of Christmas vacation traveling with his mother and trying to figure out what a student one semester away from graduating, who had withdrawn because his father had bribed his way in, should do with his life now. His heart had many ups and downs; he one day settled upon backpacking through Europe, the next on moving to a new city for a long while to "find himself," but in the end he enrolled at a local college to finish up his degree and promised to consider Poppy and Tyrone's suggestion that he join their office, at least for a time. After all, they told him, unless Elizabeth or John stepped in (and Elizabeth certainly had no desire to), the company would need to be shut down. John couldn't help feel that this was a kindness of theirs, but he accepted it nonetheless.

Elizabeth, in those few weeks, shook herself out of her funk. The death of her husband, the sudden murder of his secretary, the multitude of scandals that seemed to attach themselves to the man she had loved and known, had shaken her to her core. With the arrest of Michael, she recovered and pulled herself out of that dream-like daze that had so haunted her. At John's suggestion, when they arrived back from their travels in early February, she contacted a few art dealers and took for herself a modest position as a collector's assistant, from a woman who, after speaking with Elizabeth Eastwick for ten minutes, declared that she would need to have Elizabeth work for her to prevent her from "stealing all my business down the line."

One cold February day, just three days before John was set to start his new and final semester of college just twenty minutes down the road, John walked up to his mother's room and found her reading on her armchair, left arm curled around a mug of hot cocoa. She smiled and set down her book as she saw him, and John pulled up a seat.

For the first few weeks after Michael's arrest, it had been like they were getting reacquainted with one another: trying to understand how to act and feel after so many ugly events had occurred and uglier accusations had arisen. It turned out that Elizabeth, too, had worried about what John had done—had thought, if her son had believed his father capable of not only bribing his way into school but of having an affair and robbing him of his proper inheritance, as well, that John might have taken out his wrath on Tatiana. John was disturbed to find this out; Elizabeth was equally disturbed to find that John had thought *her* behavior suspect.

But time had softened their initial reactions, and they were back to some semblance of what they had been before—but drawn closer together in their grief, which was aching but no longer acute, for the loss of not only John Sr. but the extended family who had always existed with them in a precarious peace.

"Ready to go to the park soon?" Elizabeth said. It was the word she used for the cemetery, at which they always laid flowers on Saturday, a euphemism that rankled John some-times. But he would have patience with his mother—he knew that she, certainly, had been giving him grace in this season.

"Yes," John said. "I was thinking after we might visit Michael. From what the detectives have told me, Uncle Edward and Aunt Vanessa haven't been out there much."

"Oh, Michael," Elizabeth said, sighing. "Yes, let's. Do you think I'm allowed to bring him some cookies?"

"Maybe if they're store-bought and sealed? We can call and ask."

Elizabeth nodded, looking out the window. She had gained back a few pounds in the past few weeks: she no longer looked fragile and shriveled, but more solid, substantial. John took indescribable comfort from the change.

"I hope," she said, hesitating, still not looking at him, "I hope that you don't judge your father too harshly for anything."

"For Montvale, you mean."

Elizabeth nodded again, her gaze swinging back to John. "Whatever he did, he must have thought he was doing the best for you."

John shrugged. He had never discussed this, not since that

first day. And he didn't want to: what was the point? "He never told you anything about it? You never knew…?"

"No, John. I swear on my life." She sighed. "I wish I had a better answer for you. Your father, he—well, it just wasn't like him. He was always so rigid about rules. He paid every single parking ticket he ever got on time. I'm pretty sure we overpay on our taxes every year, just because he doesn't like any 'creative accounting,' as he likes to put it. The only thing I can think is that…"

"What?"

"I don't know. It's all speculation, dear. Maybe he was worried when you were stressed out, back in high school. Maybe he felt like he wanted to help. Maybe someone approached *him*, and he just decided to do it, and didn't think it through."

"Maybe he didn't know what he was doing," John offered.

Elizabeth smiled at him. "Maybe, darling. We don't know."

They sat in silence for some minutes. The weight of it all sat heavy upon John: he was prone, when thinking about it too much, to grow frustrated or despondent. It was the one piece he had not been able to let go, these past few weeks: he had forgiven his aunt, forgiven his uncle, had even forgiven Michael. But his father? The one person he could no longer speak to, who could no longer explain himself, take responsibility, comfort him? John did not know how to move past that.

"Does it matter?" Elizabeth said. "Would it matter to you to know?"

"Yes."

"Sometimes human hearts are unknowable," Elizabeth said, looking dreamily out the window again. "Sometimes even when we hear an explanation, it doesn't make sense."

"I'd rather know. I can't move on until I know."

Elizabeth gave him a sad, searching look. John rose to leave, no longer able to continue the conversation.

"Hold up." Elizabeth reached into her desk drawer and pulled out a letter. "This is for you. It was in your father's will."

It was a sealed letter, with John's name written across the front. He took it from her, his hand starting to tremble.

Elizabeth smiled at John. "I haven't read it. I don't know what's in there."

"How long have you had this?"

"Just a few days. Annette dropped it off before she left."

"Why did you wait to give it to me?"

"She gave them to me in an envelope—a large beige envelope. She said they were a few last documents for me to review and said to take my time. I only opened it this morning."

John still trembled, holding the letter tightly in his hands.

"Be kind," Elizabeth said. "Your father loved you."

John said nothing. His heart rate had picked up, and he took the letter from his mother and strode quickly out of the room, retreating to his bedroom to open it with no other witness. His mind spun: what if this, after all, was the letter that explained everything? What if his father acknowledged that he had bribed John's way into school, and apologized, or explained why? What if his father explained that in fact he had *not* bribed John's way into Montvale, that it was all a terrific misunderstanding, that John had no reason to feel shame?

It was neither. John read the letter once, twice, and then set it aside. He felt tears stabbing at the corners of his eyes and flicked them away. *Dear John*, it began.

I have included a letter to both you and your mother as part of this will. I want you both to know that I love you more than anything in this world, and I wish you nothing but the greatest happiness. I hope that I have had the opportunity to teach you everything that I could have; for places where I've fallen short, I trust to your intelligence, kindness, and integrity, which has always so astounded your mother and me.

You have been the greatest joy of my life, and I am a lucky man to have been the husband to your mother and a father to you. Take care of your mother, and let her take care of you.

Until we meet again,

John Eastwick Sr.

John folded the letter and put it away. Part of him felt like sobbing; part of him felt like childishly tossing the letter across the room, in rebellion against his father's untimely death, and against the answers that he would never have.

He was alone, now; his father had died, had left him. He would have to struggle forward in the world without his father's guidance, have to march blindly on without ever speaking to him again. His father was supposed to be his role model, his rock. Why had he done this? Why hadn't he explained it all away? Why hadn't it even been a big enough deal to his father that he had decided not to address it in his final letter to his son? Did he expect the secret to remain secret forever? Or did he just, simply, not care?

John's blood boiled. He wanted to turn on the fireplace and burn the letter up. He wanted to go down to his father's office and tear the letter to shreds. He wanted, more than anything else, to have his father back, for just a few minutes more.

But not long after he stood up and placed the letter lovingly inside his desk, smoothing out its edges, running his finger over the ink that his father had used to spill those words. John loved his father more than anything in the world; it had been torture to find out about Montvale, and it had been torture to think him capable of a years-long affair with Tatiana.

Now one burden was lifted, and the other remained. And would forever remain—there would be no other correspondence beyond the grave, no other messages from the late John Eastwick Sr. explaining away his mistakes in a way that would make sense to his son. He could never ask his father what was going through his mind when he made that decision. He could never hear his father's regret, or understand his father's psyche, not on this point.

He would just have to accept that his father was not perfect—that though he was the best man that John had ever known, and though he was the person that John would forever measure the rest of the world against, that he, too, had made mistakes. It was not for John to understand his father's decision. He would have to love him for what he was, and forgive him those mistakes.

He had his whole life ahead of him, after all. And as long as he lived, John Eastwick Sr. would always be alive in him.

ACKNOWLEDGMENTS

A book is never a solo effort, and I'm grateful for the many talented people that I get the privilege of working with every day.

I'd like to especially thank Alexandra and Caroline, who brought creativity, expertise, and a special kind of magic to this project.

I also want to sincerely thank Joyce and Mary, for their sharp eyes and smart commentary—I'm so lucky to have had your help.

I want to thank my family, for their eternal love and support. To my parents, you are the best humans. To my husband, thanks for your steadfast belief in me. To my siblings, I love you all so much and am proud to be your sister.

And to you, reader, thanks for showing up. I'm so grateful for you.

ALSO BY L. C. WARMAN

SNEAK PEEK OF THE LAST REAL GIRL

CHAPTER 1 OF THE LAST REAL GIRL

*B*reathtaking—that was the word they used to describe her, before and after she went missing. Charlotte Walters wasn't one of those girls that you idealized in retrospect; she was stunning, smart, charismatic, everything and anything that a seventeen-year-old wished to be. And then one day, she was gone.

That was in October. The cold had come early that year. Frost crept up the windows of our cars during the night, kissed the telephone poles at school and danced across the windows that gave melancholic views of the lake, which would soon crust over with its own layer of ice. Everything was slowing down, stiffening, draining of life. College applications were being sent in a frenzy; early admissions decisions were only six weeks away, the date ominous and foreboding. Halloween decorations had been scattered across the school, but there was something nightmarish and gaudy about them this year. They seemed, all at once, a little too real.

"Let's have a Halloween party," Charlotte said to me one day at lunch, when we had slipped out of the school to skip the whole food thing and drive for a coffee—more specifically, a pumpkin eggnog latte—which was Charlotte's latest form of dieting. She didn't need to; of course she didn't need to. She was always toothpick thin, but with just the right curves, and the delicate bone structure that gave her wrists and ankles the look of something frail and delicate and otherworldly, like a bird's. When I first met her, I used to obsess about the way she brought her long, thin hands to her teeth, chewing at the nails, fluttering like something trying to take flight. Later those nights, I would look at my own wrists, solid and flat and practical. I would try to move my hands like Charlotte's, but they only twitched like heavy spiders. I had wavy blonde hair to Charlotte's dark brown, freckled skin to her olive tones, brown eyes to Charlotte's brilliant, shocking blue. Not even our wrists, I concluded, could be alike.

"A Halloween party," I repeated, because I knew that Charlotte was not asking.

"Yes. At my house. My parents will be gone this weekend."

"What about your brother?"

"What about him? He's at state." She flicked her gaze at me, manicured fingernails drumming on the steering wheel. Most weekends this year, Aiden Walters had returned home from state, where he should have been partying and puking and altogether living up his freshman year, his first year of real freedom. Charlotte had only said, with a roll of her eyes, that he was "homesick," but I had felt the heavy atmosphere of confusion, of *wrongness*, whenever I visited Charlotte on those weekends. Charlotte's parents wore smiles even more forced than normal, and Aiden always slipped away from me. If we went to sit in the living room to watch TV, he would pick up his textbooks without a word and drift to another part of the Walters' lakeside house.

I knew better than to press further. I assumed that she had taken care of it, because Charlotte took care of everything.

"Field hockey?" I said.

"No games. States are next week. Geez, Reese, it's like

you're trying to find a reason we can't have one." Her tone was angry, but she flashed me a quick smile as we pulled into the drive thru. Charlotte ordered for both of us, two medium pumpkin eggnog lattes with whip.

"So anyway," she said, holding out her credit card to the gawking barista at the window. It was her turn to pay, a wordless rhythm that we never needed to discuss, that we fell into effortlessly. "We need decorations. Food. Booze, obviously. I think Perry will help with that."

"Maybe we can make a trip Friday to Giordano's. They have decorations and pumpkins outside. And Halloween-themed food."

"Excellent." She handed me my pumpkin latte, and a whiff of sharp cinnamon and nutmeg struck me. "Let's start working on the invite list. Party will be Saturday, at eight. So basically everyone will start showing up around nine."

"Right."

We drove back towards school, sipping on our lattes, blasting the heat our way as we rubbed cold, whitened hands on our legs to warm them up. Charlotte stretched hers in front of the air vents, cursing the chill. She said she'd probably freeze to death if she was outside longer than an hour. An image flashed into my mind, a Charlotte with pale skin and blue lips, frost crystals at the corners of her eyes. In my mind she was a frozen fay, her movements slow but still elegant, her blue eyes even sharper, wider. I shook my head.

"Oh, and Reese?" Charlotte said, as we pulled back into the school parking lot. "Don't mention anything to Mindy. About the party."

Mindy. Charlotte's co-captain on the field hockey team. The person who really should have been Charlotte's best friend, if she weren't so loyal to me. Mindy: pretty, athletic, and with a signed letter of intent to play at Dartmouth next year, because athletes and Ivy Leagues could do things their own way, not play the game of admissions letters and bureaucratic waiting.

I didn't ask why. I thought later about what would have happened if I did, if it would have changed something. Changed everything.

Instead, I just nodded.

*T*he first thing you have to understand is that nothing about Charlotte was ordinary. She had a 4.0 grade point average, had been named to the All-State team junior year, and had a talent for painting that made our art teacher, Mr. Pyrtle, cry out that Charlotte MUST pursue a career in the arts, she just MUST.

Nobody had ever told me that I needed to pursue a career in anything. But people were always trying to guide Charlotte, because Charlotte was just so full of *potential*. She could do anything, become anyone. People saw her and projected all of their dreams onto her, because she seemed like a girl who could achieve them. She would laugh about this later, pull faces to mimic those hungry voices. But I think it saddened her, a little.

That's not to say she was perfect. She wasn't going to be our valedictorian. She had taken the SAT and the ACT three times, because her parents were disappointed with her initial scores and didn't know that she had skipped her prep sessions to make out with Rex, one of the captains of the football team. She couldn't sing a tune, and she was a poor swimmer. In our mandatory P.E. class, she had in fact faked cramps for three months straight and flunked out (a doctor's note had later taken care of that). But these were minor little flaws, like salt in a sweet dish, that only brought out how utterly perfect Charlotte otherwise was.

And—yes, it was a cliché—it was hard to say no to her. Charlotte told you that she wanted something, and you moved heaven and earth to get it for her. So when she told me that Friday that she wanted a keg, a proper college keg, for the party, I promised that I would take care of it.

It took all of a couple of hours for me to realize my mistake. Charlotte could have texted any one of a dozen boys, and they would have made the same promise, except they would have *known* how to procure one. I was forced to start texting the few people whose numbers I had, begging for the same favor, with none of the charisma. At lunch, my palms were sweaty as I waited for Charlotte outside, trying to figure out if I dared to use social media to ask some other boys— who usually wouldn't spend much time talking to me, unless Charlotte were close by—if they would do this for her.

"You good?"

I jumped as a hand landed on my shoulder. I had a sudden flashing fancy of a giant scorpion, scuttling across my skin, reaching dark pincers for my neck, before the image dissipated and a pale, freckled hand withdrew. Riley. I exhaled.

"Sorry," Riley said, throwing his hands up in the air in mock surrender. His pug nose scrunched up into his face as he grinned. "You looked spooked. Guess I didn't help."

"Do you know where to get a keg?"

Riley's eyebrows shot up. I didn't care. I was desperate, at this point. Only one person had texted me back thus far, with the insulting and cutting, *Who is this?* Guess saving the side-kick's number just wasn't as important.

But Riley. Riley could do. He would have to. "Please," I said. "It's important. For a party."

I felt him studying me and blushed. I used to tutor Riley

in math, back in freshman year. It was a school program, and I needed the volunteer credits. Didn't make it any less mortifying to tutor someone my own age, a hockey player, no less, who had a quick tongue and that easy air of someone completely at home in themselves. I had had a secret, pining crush on him for three full weeks until he made out with Mindy at a party, something his friends teased him about at the learning center during our session. They had dated for two months after that, and by the time it was done I had found enough not to like about him: that rounded pug nose that I had first found cute; the way his eyes wandered when I tried to talk to him about math, looking instead for the next joke to tell or prank to pull; the height that was only an inch or two more than mine; and finally, finally, that even though he waved to me in the hall and said hi in front of his friends, he never straightened up or preened the way he did when he saw a girl like Charlotte pass by.

One day, I thought, I'd find someone who preferred me to Charlotte.

But right now I didn't need a boyfriend or a declaration of undying, Charlotte-free love. I needed a keg.

"A party," Riley repeated. I noticed he had a math worksheet clutched in one hand—the real reason he had approached me. "This Charlotte's Halloween party?"

"Yes."

"Am I invited? Don't worry," he said, as I visibly tensed. "We already got the invites."

"We?"

"Hockey team." He grinned. "You need to relax more."

I hated it when people told me that. "So can you help?"

"Yeah, I can help. Now?"

I clapped my hands together before my brain could catch up and prevent such idiocy. "Oh, thank you," I said, and just managed to prevent myself from reaching out to hug him.

"Really, thank you. Tomorrow at noon? We can bring it to Charlotte's house beforehand."

"I'll just bring it when we come, sound good?"

"Oh—oh, sure. I'll get you the money tomorrow." My hands flapped around my wallet, but I knew I didn't have the cash on me. Besides, how much did a keg cost anyway? Twenty dollars? Forty dollars?

"Great. Hey, could I bother you to take a look at this?"

It was as I leaned over Riley's math assignment that the thought crept to me, slow and needling: if Charlotte had asked him, he would have pretended to need her the whole day. He'd have driven her around looking at all sorts of kegs, just to spend some more time with her. With girls like Charlotte, boys squeezed every drop they could. With me, it was all business, all transaction.

A car horn honked. "Here," I said, snatching the pen from Riley's hand as I glanced up at Charlotte, who was tossing back her hair as she adjusted her rearview mirror. She gave the car another honk for good measure, and someone behind her in the traffic circle answered with one of their own. She flipped them off and waved again at me.

I wrote out the math problem in a hurried scribble for Riley. "You can do the rest that way," I said. "You have to factor the terms—here, and here. You see?"

But Riley was staring at Charlotte. Of course he was. He took the pen and paper from me absentmindedly.

"Do you want to go to the party?" Riley asked, as I swung my bag over my shoulder.

"What?"

Riley shook himself, as if coming to. "Nothing," he murmured. He gave me a quick grin as Charlotte laid on the horn again. "Just thought someone like you would prefer math homework to a party."

"Sorry to disappoint, but I'll be there," I said. It had meant to come out joking and light, to match his tone, but there was a little too much realness to it. It poured from my mouth bitter and hot, and Riley blinked up at me, his expression changing. Mortified, I spun around and hopped in the car, cheeks burning.

"How's our favorite albino mountain troll?" Charlotte said, zipping out onto the road.

"He's bringing a keg tomorrow."

"Oh, lovely! My savior. Hey," she said, as she braked hard at the red light, sending us careening forward against our seatbelts. "You know what's spooky? Ghosts. Like Cassandra Lewis."

I glanced sideways at Charlotte. Cassandra Lewis was a thick, gorilla-looking girl with a bad unibrow and a slow, pitiful gaze. She had disappeared a few months ago from school, and Charlotte had been one of the only people to notice. Charlotte was like that; she paid attention even when you thought she wasn't. Most people figured Cassandra's parents had sent her to boarding school, or else switched to homeschooling, but Charlotte had insisted on going by the house to find out. I had looked up the address in the directory with her. Turned out the parents had clean moved out, which disappointed Charlotte; it meant that Cassandra had likely moved, and not been kidnapped or murdered or abducted by aliens, as would make the better story.

"They still might have left out of grief," Charlotte had said hopefully, and I had murmured some form of agreement.

But now I only waited as Charlotte drove on, humming slightly to herself, looking mischievous and a little pleased. "The theme," Charlotte announced, as she took a sharp curve onto a side road, "will be ghosts. Ghosts of dead girls, in fact."

"Is that a theme?"

"Of course it's a theme."

"Okay, so… You want me to bring some extra bedsheets?"

Charlotte laughed, throwing her head back so far that I almost wanted to grab the wheel from her. "You wait and see," she said. "My place at three tomorrow. You're going to help me bake cookies."

"Ghost-shaped, I hope?"

Charlotte grinned. But just as quickly it faded. The shadows on her face, mottled and shifting as the sun broke through the passing leaves, looked like writhing snakes on her skin.

The silence lasted for one minute, then another. Charlotte looked serious, and the suddenness of the change threw me.

"Reese," she said finally, voice low, "do you sometimes think there's something *wrong* with St. Clair?"

"St. Clair?" I said, the name of our town sweet and sharp like a bell in my mouth. St. Clair was beautiful. Picturesque. A kid like Charlotte probably took it for granted, idealized it, hated it because someone with money could. Could actually think that they might escape to a big city one day, away from the suburban glamor and old-money confidence of a place like our lakeside town. Could laugh away the four or five or nine generations of Walters who had lived there before her, because they were like stone weights around her neck, because she didn't know what it was like to come to St. Clair at eleven and be forced to live among a set of students who took for granted that your parents were together, that they vacationed in Aspen, that they looked down with cloying suffocation on anyone who lived "beyond the hill."

"Sometimes," Charlotte said, "I think we're all a little crazy here."

I responded with a noise that might have been either assent or dissent.

"Except for you," Charlotte said. "You're not. Not yet."

*W*e spent most of that day shopping and decorating; Charlotte had field hockey practice Saturday morning, and so I was tasked with picking up some of the harder-to-find items that we had missed Friday. I used my mom's car to putter first to the market, and then to the Halloween store, the latter surrounded by an explosion of pumpkins and white cobweb fuzz that made it hard to walk without getting entangled in something.

And then noon came, and I was out of things to do, and I had missed two calls from my mother already. I considered going to a coffee shop and sitting down with a maple latte, perhaps doing a little bit of the homework I had in my backpack. But no; my mother's hospital shift started soon, and as much as we argued and fought for control of the car, I wasn't stupid or selfish enough to think that my joyriding came before her work.

I timed my arrival late enough that my mother had only the opportunity to deliver a few sharp words before she took the keys and reversed out of the driveway. I watched her go, her thick wavy hair plaited in a severe braid down her back, her freckled skin bagged and wrinkled from the stress of her job, from me, from the unforgiving winters in St. Clair. I wondered for a moment if she still told people she was from Florida; I had stopped doing so years ago, when I felt that the land of crabgrass and sunshine no longer had a tight hold on me. But I suppose for her, it would always be home. St. Clair was exile.

I lugged in my bags and fended off the whining, excited overtures from Morty, our shepherd rescue. He bounced left and right and forward and back as I deposited the bags on the counter, chasing his white tail, then coming to a low crouch, then bounding across the room and leaping up onto our green sofa. "I know," I said. "Groceries are quite exciting."

Morty barked his agreement.

My mother had never really told me why we had to move, all those years ago. I tried to picture it as I packed up the decorations and moved some perishables into the fridge. I had come home from school one day, sticky and warm from the sun, and she had sat me down with a lopsided smile. "Guess what, darling?" she had said. "We're moving north!"

"To Jacksonville?" I said. My mother had friends there; she'd often talk wistfully about it.

"Jacksonville? Oh, no! No, darling, much further. Right near Canada, actually."

At this point, my mother used to tell me, I broke down and started crying, saying I didn't want to be Canadian. That's not how I remember it: I remember talking quite calmly about whether we were to become Canadians, and learning that no, we would be moving to a lakeside town on the outskirts of a city, with a great hospital program for my mother. I think she had talked then of more schooling, of a degree program or specialized training of some sort, but if that's why we moved it never panned out; my mother had the same job she always did, tough but reliable, demanding but impressive. And a few months in, she began dating Jerry, a local tax accountant, who left her for a hairdresser three years later and then moved her and his two apple-faced children to Denver.

I thought about Charlotte's question the night before: *Do you think there's something* wrong *with St. Clair?* If there was, I couldn't see it, at least not on the surface. The entire place was out of a storybook. Most of the city was grids of manicured houses with freshly cut lawns and medians, perfectly square sidewalks and oak and maple trees lining the wide streets. The houses were all brick or white stone, with wrought-iron gates and little detached garages. And that was only on the regular side of town—go east, towards the water, and the flat idyllic land and cute little downtown transformed into rolling hills and wooded roads, like you were entering some kind of fairy tale. It was here where the rich of the rich lived, in castle-like houses on the shore, overlooking the wide and dark lake. It was here where Charlotte's family lived, in a house fit for royalty, with a driveway half a mile long and a balcony off the master where we'd have coffee and whiskey the mornings when Mr. and Mrs. Walters were gone, kicking our feet through the stone balustrades and talking about tales of kids who had once tried to swim across the lake.

I shook myself and looked at the clock. Still another two hours to kill. I pulled out my homework, made some instant coffee, and plunged onto the sofa, where Morty hopped up and immediately rested his chestnut head on my thigh. I petted him absently. My pen hovered over my trig problems, and my eyes darted between our warped floors, our cracked fireplace, and the perpetually dew-covered windows of our little townhouse. It was a nice place to live; I knew it was, I was grateful for it, and my mother certainly reminded me of our landlord's kindness in keeping rent stable all these years (they were both single mothers, and at various times I had to be subjected to awkward dinners with Mrs. Leaventrott, who would wear pearls and a patterned flower dress and size me up with her cataract-clouded eyes, trying to decide if I was the type of girl who deserved her continued charity).

But our home was nothing compared to Charlotte's—and I'm not talking about the rent vs. own divide. I knew I shouldn't be jealous. I knew that envy could be ugly, caustic, eating up your insides with its insidious whispers of how much you deserved and how little everyone else did. But my jealousy was of a different nature. I did not begrudge Charlotte her wonders. I was amazed that she had chosen to share them with me.

The story was always so fascinating to people, but the truth was, it was simple: Charlotte was rich and pretty and charismatic. At a certain point in middle school, her friends turned against her. And then I came to town: a blank slate, a fresh start. Charlotte cleaved to me. Even when the girls came around, even when they wanted her back, Charlotte never abandoned our friendship. She knew she could trust me more than all of those girls put together, and we were best friends the moment she sat down at my empty table in middle school, offered me half of a peanut butter sandwich, and said, "I need new friends. Are you interested?"

I was.

When I arrived at Charlotte's a little past three, she shouted down the wide stair banister in the two-floor entryway that she would be down in a few minutes. "Face mask!" she shouted, by way of explanation, before the door slammed shut.

I moved to the kitchen and began unloading supplies. Charlotte already had the ghost cookie cutters laid out for us to use; I found myself amused and then a little excited at the ridiculousness of the theme.

I was about to toss the eggs in the fridge when I paused. Taped on the outside of the fridge was a photo of the family.

Charlotte's mother, tall and slim and blonde, with Charlotte's striking blue eyes and tilted cheekbones. Charlotte's father, broad-shouldered and beaming, arm draped proudly across the back of his wife and two kids. Charlotte, in a long slip of a black dress, dark hair draped luxuriously across her shoulders, expression sweet but also a little wicked, like she was laughing at you behind the camera. And then her brother, Aiden.

I stepped closer.

His expression was odd. Like the camera had caught him by surprise. His brows were furrowed, his mouth puckered, and his hands were thrust deep into his pockets, as though he wished to disappear. There was something urgent about him. For a moment I imagined him stepping outside of the photograph, pulling his hands out of his pockets to stretch them out towards me. "Listen," he would say, "you have to know—"

"What are you doing?"

I startled. Some of the eggs tumbled from the carton and landed with a sickening *splat* on the hardwood below, gooey yolk oozing across the floorboards. I quickly placed the rest of the carton on the counter and began to flutter about looking for paper towels, my face a burning red. I felt rather than saw Aiden sigh and put down his bag, and tear off a sheet to help me.

"Sorry," he said gruffly, pulling out a spray bottle of lemon floor cleaner from beneath the sink. "I shouldn't have startled you."

I risked a glance up at him. The animosity still had not left his voice. His expression was hardly much friendlier. It was always trippy to look at him; he was the spitting image of Charlotte (I'd forever think of it that way, even though Aiden was a year older). He had the same dark hair, the same bright blue eyes and tilted cheekbones, the same elegant hands. He was more solid though, more real and less fairy, with the broadness of his father and a height about six inches taller than his willowy sister. I knew plenty of girls in our grade who had been obsessed with him, and I was convinced that it was at least half of the reason why, all those years ago, Charlotte had been welcomed back into their good graces. Aiden had been a lacrosse player, and had even had some offers to play D3 in various out-of-state prestigious liberal arts colleges. I didn't know why he had chosen state; I had always assumed that it was because it was the natural choice for almost everyone who could get in. It was most likely where I was going, next year—though that was because I couldn't afford to carry loans from anywhere else.

"Here," I said, taking the dirty paper towels from him as he set to work on the final splooch. I deposited them into the Walters' kitchen trash, in the tub hidden away in a soft-closing cabinet. Aiden rubbed the last spot and straightened, jerking right to throw the rest of the paper towels away.

"I thought you would be gone this weekend," I blurted out, and then blushed as his gaze turned towards me.

I found myself unable to hold the gaze for very long, and instead my eyes flickered over his long-sleeved T-shirt, his polo shorts, his loafers. Was that hate I could feel radiating off of him? Aiden had always been polite but distant towards me, but something had changed since last summer. Something that had made him cool towards everyone, that had made his presence something heavy and uncomfortable, almost awkward. Charlotte wouldn't talk about it, and I couldn't very well ask anyone else what had happened. I supposed he had gotten in trouble, somehow. That his weekends home were penance for some unknown sin.

"I'm here every weekend," Aiden said finally. "It's my house."

"Well, of course, I didn't mean that," I said, flushing again. I forced myself to meet his gaze, even though it only made me turn redder. "I just—well, are you coming to the party?"

"Not if I can help it."

Right, then. "Well, have a good day," I said, turning my shoulders so that I no longer faced him. I put the remainder of eggs in the fridge and began to busy myself again; no need to continue to try to talk to him if that's how he was going to play it. I wondered if he was rude because he thought I was weird for staring at his family portrait. It *was* weird, but then, who wouldn't be curious?

"Have a good time at the party," Aiden said. There was something in his voice, some catch that I couldn't quite make out. "Sorry for startling you." His footsteps retreated across the hardwood, and then up the stairs. I heard a bright "Hello, brother!" and the click of Charlotte's heels on the floor before the fresh-faced Charlotte appeared in front of me and spun around twice, laughing. She had on a T-shirt and plain shorts, and snatched up a long apron.

"Cookie time!" she said, and for a moment she was not seventeen-year-old Charlotte, hauntingly gorgeous, dangerously cunning, but the Charlotte of middle school, playful and mischievous and full of easy smiles. I caught the apron she tossed towards me and tied it on.

Charlotte chatted easily on about the guest list for the night, which was large enough that it was apparent it would get out of control. She talked about the handful of football players who were blowing up her phone that afternoon, who assumed, like all boys did who were interested in her, that she must have orchestrated the whole event specially for them. She told me the string of gossip she had heard about last night —parties attended, couples formed and dissolved, girls ditched and boys slighted. I knew rationally that she had learned it all over text, that many people in the school felt gossip wasn't real until Charlotte Walters knew about it, but another part of me felt that the source of her knowledge was deeper, more mysterious, that Charlotte Walters knew everything because she *was* the town, or everything that St. Clair liked to think of itself as. I imagined roots growing down from her feet, expanding out beneath the cold earth, poking up in every house, school, and building and glittering in the frost and ice of late October.

"By the way," she said, as we cut the last of the sugar cookies from the dough and arranged it on the sheet, "I hear Riley has a thing for you. Just be careful. You know, those hockey guys." Her hand flicked in some dismissive motion, and I went very still. I didn't know Aiden was behind me until he reached around to grab the filtered water on the counter.

"No one's staying past two," Aiden said, pouring himself a cup. "And I'm not covering for you if the police are called."

Charlotte rolled her eyes and flashed me a smile, which I returned weakly. At the very least, I thought, the interruption had saved me from having to respond to her warning. Riley? No, she had it all wrong. I thought about the way he had looked at her as she had driven up, the way his gaze followed her that afternoon. It wouldn't be the first time someone had pretended to be interested in me to get in Charlotte's good graces; it was short-sighted and stupid, but you really couldn't expect much more out of high school boys.

"The police won't be called. We're a half mile from anyone else. Who's going to make the noise complaint?"

"It's happened before."

Charlotte again waved her hand dismissively. I felt Aiden's gaze light on me again, and I met it, not wanting to be intimidated. He seemed to be considering something. His mouth opened, then closed.

"Take a picture, it will last longer," Charlotte said, and then snickered when Aiden gave her the finger and left.

I wondered what it was that Aiden had wanted to say.

*T*he party was in full swing by eight o'clock; for Charlotte Walters' parties, there was no fashionably late. No one wanted to miss a moment.

Riley had arrived right on time with the keg. I could feel Charlotte watching us as I let him in, and so I was brusquer than normal, business-like. I asked him a few times how much the keg cost, and he demurred politely once, then twice, before telling me. I handed him the cash, all my wages that were to last me this week and next—my next library paycheck would not be until the Friday after.

Riley hesitated when I held out the cash, but Charlotte was nearby, hanging a few cobweb decorations, and so I smacked the money on the counter and pretended to go busy myself elsewhere. Sure enough, a few moments later Riley was asking Charlotte about the theme of the party, and I was forgotten. No matter. Charlotte wouldn't be interested in someone like him, anyway.

I nursed one cup of beer for those first few hours; my mother was like a bloodhound, and I knew that if I had much more she would sniff it out on me and ground me for weeks. She wasn't the kind of mother who served wine at dinner like the Walters, or who let their children drink so long as it was in the house. Once, last year, I had even seen Mrs. Walters hand Charlotte a cigarette, mother and daughter standing on the top balcony, looking out at the lake as they blew matching puffs of smoke into the wind. I had been on my way out after a sleepover, and the image had stayed with me for months; when I closed my eyes, sometimes I could still see it, the two elegant figures draped over the balustrade, elven ghosts that were as wispy as their smoky breaths.

Mindy, Charlotte's field hockey co-captain, ended up coming after all, as of course Charlotte knew that she would. The important thing was that Mindy had not been invited specifically, that she knew she was not technically welcome. I could see it in the stiff way that Mindy entered the house, flanked by her field hockey friends, the way she laughed too loud at the first joke thrown at her, the way she beelined for the blood-red punch with floating rubber spiders and poured herself a portion before emptying a whiskey nip into it.

I was sitting on the couch in the living room, the black leather L-shaped one that faced the fireplace and the giant TV, on which was playing the tail end of one of the state football games. I could smell cigar smoke wafting in from the patio, and when I turned my head and craned it over the patches of kids sitting and leaning against every available surface, I could make out Charlotte talking to Danny, a football player, as Mindy skulked nearby. Charlotte had on a slinking white dress with a slit up the side; Mindy, in white behind her, looked like some squashed-down version of Charlotte, half a foot shorter and wider, solid. It was odd, because Mindy was a very pretty girl—funny, too, so everyone liked her and she had more than half the class in love with her. But no one could stand next to Charlotte Walters and look good, except, perhaps, another Walters.

"Let's go to the couch," Charlotte said, as Mindy hovered a step closer, presumably to greet Charlotte, to see for herself whether the snub had been intentional. Danny followed Charlotte to a spot near me, and a few juniors immediately cleared out to make room. "Danny, you know Reese? Reese, Danny."

I nodded at him, though we had met twice before, and he smiled and shook my hand before spinning back to Charlotte.

"You know," Charlotte said, getting up and depositing herself between Danny and me, so she could turn her mischievous gaze my way and turn her shoulder away from Danny, "the last owners of this house told us that the property was haunted."

I felt a prickle at the back of my neck. We'd talked about this before, a couple times, mostly when Charlotte was bored. She would ask me if I believed in ghosts, if I thought that a chill in the air meant some other presence was in the room with you, if I thought that creaking doors and flickering lights could mean anything. I played the scoffing skeptic, starkly unwilling to believe any of that hocus pocus, but in truth it creeped me out, and I would always spend the night after with the lamp on next to my bed, falling asleep in the orange glow because otherwise the shadows were too much for me, the whispers and rustles too loud.

"Haunted?" Danny said, miffed at Charlotte's cold shoulder but not ready to give up yet. His curly black hair flopped over his forehead, and he pushed it back with one of those textbook teenage neck jerks to toss it ineffectually—for just a moment—back over his head. "Like hocus pocus?" He wiggled his hands, and Charlotte rolled her eyes.

"Sure, like hocus pocus," she said. She cast a glance at me, inviting me to share in her amusement. But I didn't have the social capital to laugh at someone like Danny, so I only smiled gently and tucked one leg underneath me. "You remember when you were sleeping over that night, Reese, and we heard those clinks in the kitchen?"

"Someone was getting a midnight snack," Danny said. "I do it all the time."

"Oh yeah? What about the fact that we were the only ones in the house that night?" This was not strictly true—Charlotte's mother had been there. But she slept like the dead, and so it might as well have been.

"Well," Danny said, grinning, pleased that he had coaxed Charlotte's attention back his way, "maybe it was just someone passing through." He grew mock sober. "However, if you're worried and would like someone to stay the night, stand watch—"

Charlotte snorted, but she let Danny throw one arm over her shoulder. I felt a few heads near us turn, the whispers start as a potential pairing surfaced. I wanted to tell them not to bother; it wouldn't last. But instead I rested my chin on my knee and looked up at Charlotte, waiting.

"So who died, then?" Danny said, lowering his voice, but not by much. I could feel others listening in. Danny wanted me to go; that was plain. And I'd be more than happy to. I didn't want to play chaperone, didn't want Charlotte to use me to build tension with this new guy, pretending she had to be a good friend (*oh, but she's sitting all alone*) and spend time with me, all because she never intended to give him what he was after.

"An old man," Charlotte said. "And his wife. The people before us said that he probably killed her."

"Doesn't seem like a great way to sell real estate." Riley deposited himself next to me on the couch, offering me an unopened can of beer. I took it, because it was something to do with my hands, and murmured a thanks. Danny gave him a quick look, assessing the threat.

"Well, they told us after we had bought it, naturally," Charlotte said. "My mom reached out about all of the weird sounds, and that's when they told us."

"Too late to back out, I guess," Danny said.

"Oh, all the contracts around here have provisions in them about ghosts. You didn't know that? You're not allowed to cancel a contract, or sue for that matter, because of ghostly activity."

"That can't be true," I protested.

"It is." Riley swirled the beer around in his own can. "My mom's a realtor. Some leftover clause from the eighteenth century, or something."

A realtor? I hadn't known that. I wondered what Riley's dad did, but I didn't want to ask. The question would always come back to me, and I'd have to say that my dad lived out in New Mexico and was a contractor. Only half of it was true, or at least based on truth—the last child support check my mother had gotten had been from New Mexico, but my father had never done a day's hard labor in his life. He was a trust-fund kid who had partied hard, young, and flirted briefly with monogamy when he met my mother before abandoning it, and us, entirely. I had never whined or complained about this, or threatened my mom that I wanted to go live with him, because it was plainly apparent that in him we had a common enemy, someone who had disrupted her life and catapulted mine into existence, and then disappeared after the explosion, to leave us to pick up the pieces.

"Really?" Charlotte said, shaking me out of my reverie. I was glad, because I noticed then that Riley was studying my expression, that I had maybe let a little too much slip. "That's awesome. Has she seen any haunted houses, then?"

"People have claimed it, here and there. She doesn't really believe in that stuff."

"Doesn't matter if you believe it or not, if it's true," Charlotte said, grinning at him. Danny bristled.

"So an old man," he said. "Kind of a boring ghost. What does he do, complain about his bunions all night?"

"And what would an *interesting* ghost be?" Charlotte asked, turning towards him.

Danny grinned. There was something artificial about it, about both of them actually, that threw me. "Ever heard of

Screaming Stella? Out on that island in the middle of St. Clair. If you go out at midnight, on a full moon, you can hear her—"

"Oh, *can* you?"

"It's a full moon tonight," Danny teased. Of course it was. He knew that beforehand. Next thing he was going to tell her was that she could only hear it while skinny-dipping in the water. "We could go out, if you don't believe me."

"And Screaming Stella is—?"

"A young girl who was murdered out there. Probably in like, the 50s, or something."

"Ah," Charlotte said, turning with a wink towards me. "Of course. A young, beautiful girl. It always is."

"It always is what?" Danny said.

"Someone young and beautiful. America is OBSESSED with dead girls," Charlotte said. She cut her gaze sideways towards me. "If I died, Reese, would you be obsessed with me?"

I opened my mouth, paused. "Yes" didn't seem right. "No" didn't either. And I didn't have a witty rejoinder ready.

"So this Screaming Stella," Riley said, saving me from a response. "You hear her at what, midnight?"

"Midnight, lakeside," Danny said. I could have sworn for a moment that I saw fear flash across his face, as if he actually believed this stuff. "And this house is close to the lake—it can't be what, more than a quarter of a mile there?"

Charlotte looked down at her drink. There suddenly seemed something off about her, I thought. Her face was a little gray, her expression pinched. She seemed to be shrinking, withdrawing into herself, even as all the eyes of our little group turned upon her. I heard someone behind us loudly suggest a game of spin the bottle, and another searing voice dismiss him. And there was Charlotte, the beating heart of the party, shriveling.

Then she drew her head back up, and the illusion

vanished. She was Charlotte again—brave, reckless, beautiful. "What do you think, Reese?" she said, grinning.

I wasn't going to be the party pooper. "I think we should go," I said. "Let's see if there's any truth in it."

Danny and Charlotte exchanged a glance. Again I felt that odd sense that I was the outsider here, that something else was between them that I couldn't touch. And then Charlotte looked away.

In the next couple of days, I'd replay this scene in my head, over and over. Trying to figure out how it could have gone differently—how it could have been stopped.

End of Sample

AFTERWORD

Thank you for reading! To stay up-to-date on L.C. Warman's new releases, subscribe to Greenleaf & Plympton's newsletter.

Greenleaf & Plympton is a boutique publisher of gothic novels, both modern and classic.

By "gothic," we specifically mean books of murder, mystery, and magic. These books include some or all of the following characteristics:

- A mystery
- A tinge of the supernatural, a hint of magic, or just some sense that there is something more out there
- A sense of nostalgia, or of the past haunting the present
- A deep focus on character
- A style that is literary, but still accessible

These gothic books are NOT necessarily dark and dreary. They often couple a spooky atmosphere with cutting humor, or a sense of whimsy. They're not overly gory or violent, even though they may involve murder, disappearances, and battles.

Some of the recurring themes you might find in these books include:

- Old estates
- Family secrets
- Secret societies
- Criminal underworlds/black markets
- Blackmail
- Murder mysteries
- Trains, clocks, maps, and more
- Isolated hotels
- Old universities
- Mysterious figures
- Mistaken identities
- Circuses and magic shows
- Fortune-telling
- etc.

Are you just as big a fan of these books as us? Sign up to join our community of gothic book lovers, where we share exclusive stories, send letters both print and digital, and give you a gift on your birthday.

You can also browse our catalog of available gothic books at https://www.greenleafandplympton.com.

Welcome! We're so glad you found us.

by L.C. Warman
The Last Real Girl (Book 1)
The Last Real Crime (Book 2)
The Last Real Secret (Book 3)

All of our modern titles are available in ebook and paperback. Find our full list of available titles by visiting https://greenleafandplympton.com.

Website: *https://greenleafandplympton.com*

instagram.com/greenleafandplympton

ABOUT THE AUTHOR

L.C. Warman is the author of spooky young adult mysteries. She grew up in New England, in a town where real estate contracts stipulated that you couldn't back out if you discovered your new place was haunted. She currently lives in a Michigan lakeside town with her husband and two dogs.